BETTER THAN A BOX OF CHOCOLATES

A NOVELLA

EMILY MARCH

EMILY MARCH BOOKS

Published by Emily March Books.

ISBNs 978-1-942002-61-1 (paperback) 978-1-942002-59-8 (ebook)

CHAPTER 1

Dallas, Texas

Ali Lovejoy cruised along I30 headed west in her sweet little Mercedes convertible listening to classic rock on the car stereo. Hoping to catch a traffic report as she headed home toward Fort Worth, she sang along with The Boss until the final notes of "Born To Run" faded into an all-too-familiar jingle. Then, quick as a rattlesnake, she struck the preset button to change the station before the teddy bear advertisement blared from her speakers.

"…send lovely red roses, delivery guaranteed…."

Her index finger poked again.

"…delicious chocolate-covered strawberries…."

Jab.

"…peek-a-boo pajamas to your Valentine today!"

This time, Ali hit the "off" button. She'd rather risk bumper-to-bumper traffic than listen to one more of those commercials.

Not that she had anything against stuffed animals or flowers or sexy lingerie or chocolate anything, because she didn't. In fact, Ali was a big fan of romance.

It paid the bills.

Ali made her living as a wedding photographer. This very moment she was on her way home from signing a lucrative contract with a MOB—aka mother-of-the-bride—to photograph all of the events surrounding her daughter's June nuptials.

Romance was good for Ali's bottom line.

Valentine's Day made her cranky.

The day of red hearts and roses had been a source of trouble for her for much of her life, from Kindergarten's decorated shoeboxes to last year's one-for-the-record-books humiliating Valentine's Day. Now, during this first week of February, all she wanted to do was play Rip Van Winkle and hide under the covers until February 17th.

She tacked on a few extra days to allow bargain shoppers to clear the shelves of discounted chocolates, which was a real sacrifice because Ali did adore her chocolate.

The touch screen on her dashboard signaled an incoming call. Recognizing the number, Ali smiled as she answered. "Jessica! Well? Was the shopping trip a success? Did you say yes to a dress?"

"No!" Her best friend and college roommate replied with a groan in her voice. "I found some 'maybes,' but nothing that screamed 'This is the one.' My mom is getting frustrated with me."

"I can't imagine why. You've only tried on, what? Six hundred wedding gowns?"

Jessica sniffed. "No more than five hundred fifty."

"Well, no rush. You still have plenty of time."

"Speaking of time, that's why I'm calling. I have a huge favor to ask."

Uh oh. If Jessica Martingale said it was a big favor, it would be a big favor, and Ali would be obligated to grant it.

After all, if not for Jessica going above and beyond when Ali came down with mononucleosis during their last semester at the University of Texas, Ali wouldn't have graduated on time. And her friend had been her rock many other times since.

Her friend continued. "Ordinarily, I wouldn't dream of suggesting this because it's a huge ask. But under the circumstances, I think it could be a win/win for both of us. Sean will be happy because a relative of his is pushing for it. Something to do with a distant, elderly aunt. I admit I don't understand that part, but the Gallaghers are a huge family, and I haven't met everyone. Of course, I'll understand if you can't do it, and my feelings won't be hurt or anything. I just want it to be you so bad because you're the best photographer in the entire world, and you're my maid of honor, and we could have a really fun long weekend."

"Jessica. Jessica. Slow down. I gather you want me to photograph something? That's not a big ask."

"I haven't told you the who, what, where, and when."

Ali waited. And waited. And waited. "Jessica?"

She asked in a rush. "Will you come to Colorado and photograph the reenactment of my Christmas Eve engagement?"

"You jerk!" Ali exclaimed, slamming on her brakes to avoid hitting the florist delivery van that abruptly changed lanes in front of her.

"Oh."

Hearing the hurt in her former roomie's voice, Ali quickly explained. "Not you, goose. I was talking to the idiotic driver in front of me. Of course I'll take your engagement photos. I'd be honored, in fact. The problem is my schedule. You know I work almost every weekend."

"That's the 'when' part. I know you aren't working this

particular weekend because you've sworn a blood oath that you're not leaving your house."

Oh. Ali's stomach sank. She knew what was coming.

Jessica continued, "This year, Valentine's Day falls on a Saturday. So we're doing the reenactment on Valentine's weekend."

Okay, that is a big ask.

Ali had spent the past twelve months padding a lawyer's bank account while she put the pieces of her heart back together. Approaching the first anniversary of the death of her dreams on the worst day of the year was bad enough. The last thing she wanted or needed was to risk running into her Valentine's Nightmare Past. But unfortunately, the way her luck ran, that's precisely what would happen.

And yet, this was Jessica doing the asking, and the venue was a small, isolated mountain town in Colorado. The odds of running into her ex in Eternity Springs were next to nil, and she could still follow through with her current Valentine's evening plans from there. So doing this favor for her bestie wouldn't break her vow in any way. In fact, it might be good to get out of the house.

"Cool. I'm free on Valentine's weekend. I can watch horror movies on the night of the fourteenth in a hotel room as easily as I can in my own bedroom."

"Horror movies? You don't watch horror movies."

"It's a new tradition of mine I've decided to establish in keeping with the spirit of the holiday."

Jessica laughed. "Oh, Ali. You're a mess. Well, we will be staying at Sean's family's bed-and-breakfast in Eternity Springs. They might have a theater room. If you're serious about this new tradition, I'll reserve it for you. I've been warned that we need to make reservations for everything we want to do while we're in town because there's a hot air balloon festival that weekend, and the place is packed."

Ali's artistic interest perked up. She tried to recall what Jessica had told her about the place where she'd gotten engaged. She had a mental vision of a Victorian snow village, and the hot air balloons didn't fit it. "I'm intrigued. Isn't there a lake in this little town?"

"Yes. Hummingbird Lake. I think the balloons take off from there."

"Cool. That's something I'd like to watch if we have time."

"You'll definitely have time. The balloon flights take place at dawn. It won't be interfering with anything I have scheduled."

Ali laughed at that little truth. Jessica was not a morning person. The two women discussed their travel schedules until Ali heard an electronic sound in the call's background. Jessica said, "Gotta go. Class is about to start."

"Go whip those Kindergarteners into shape, Miss Martingale."

"I'll try. I swear this year's group is five going on twenty-five. I'll email you the deets about your reservation at Aspen-glow Place B&B. Bye!"

"Aspenglow Place B&B," Ali repeated softly as she checked her mirrors and switched lanes. Didn't that sound inviting? And a winter balloon festival—bet she could get some glorious shots. She hadn't done any outdoor photography in way too long. It'd be a nice change.

And so, to Ali's complete and utter amazement, she found herself looking forward to the second weekend in February. The drive to her destination from her home in Fort Worth could be made in one long, hard day of driving, but she preferred to get an early start and break it into two.

The trip required using her work vehicle, a four-wheel-drive SUV with plenty of storage space for all of her equipment. So, the night before her departure, she loaded the SUV, then set her alarm for Zero-Dark-Thirty and crawled into bed.

Ali dreamed about drinking Earl Gray tea with a tiny, elderly woman who had crystalline blue eyes and the lilt of Ireland in her voice.

Weird.

CHAPTER 2

Eternity Springs, Colorado

Max Romano peeked through his office blinds and gazed down into the tasting room at the Tipsy Angel Microbrewery. "What are all these people doing here? All these women!"

Lying at his feet, Barney, his coal-black Newfoundland and best friend, thumped his tail twice.

"It's a Thursday in February!" Max continued. "We should have one customer, two at the most. And they should be locals!"

Max's sister, Gabriella Romano Brogan, propped her long legs atop his desk and crossed them at the ankles. With her right hand, she idly scratched her own Newfoundland, Bismarck, behind the ears. Gabi's brilliant blue eyes gleamed with amusement as she observed, "That's a terrible attitude for a business owner, brother dear."

"Yeah, well. You try walking around Eternity Springs in my shoes for the past week or so."

"You mean because of the rumor floating around that our famous cousin, Luscious Lorenzo, is in town? That's why you asked me to take Barney on a walk with Bismarck instead of walking him yourself, isn't it? You're afraid to show your pretty face around town?"

"It's not fear. It's self-preservation. And I'm not pretty."

Gabi giggled-snorted. "Sure, you're not."

Max scowled over his shoulder at his sister. "I'm glad you think this is so funny. I'm not the only person catching flack, by the way. Flynn needs to stay on his guard. You've told me women find that eyepatch he wears sexy."

At the mention of her husband, Gabi's laughter died. She yanked her feet off the desk and sat up straight. "Did somebody bother Flynn?"

"Not that I know of, but I'm afraid it's just a matter of time. The crazies went after Cicero yesterday."

"Cicero! Why? What happened? He didn't say anything to me."

"He was probably afraid you'd pull out your old sheriff's uniform and go looking for the free-handed floozies yourself."

"Free-handed floozies? What is this, the 1930's?"

"One of them ripped my shirt! Another went for my junk."

"Seriously? Okay, start at the beginning, Max."

"Fine." Barney's tail gave a hard thump against the floor in support. Max continued. "Cicero and I met for coffee at the Mocha Moose and stood in line next to some people who are in town with the balloon festival. They didn't believe me when I denied I was Lorenzo, and Cicero thought it would be cute to stir the pot, and he joked around."

"I mean, as far as jokes go, it's actually pretty clever."

"Not helpful." He scowled. "Anyway, before you know it, these three women have us backed up against the wall. And then two of them come at me trying to manhandle me! It wasn't a pleasant situation."

"Oh, dear."

"Yeah. So, that's why I asked you to walk Barney for me this morning. Even with a mountain of a dog at my side, I'm wary of showing my face in public right now."

Disgust lacing her voice, Gabi wondered, "What is wrong with people? I know Lorenzo's the star of a number one Netflix series, but is that really enough reason for people to lose their minds?"

"I blame social media for everything. Anyway, I also need you to call Lorenzo and convince him that he needs to get splashy for the paparazzi. I don't care where he is. He needs to draw the heat away from Eternity Springs. I would call him, but he'd go to ground just out of spite. You always had more influence with Lorenzo than I did."

"That's because I didn't break his nose when he was twelve."

"He deserved the punch. He knows it. Come on, Gabi. I'm begging you. You have to convince him to do this. Remind him that he owes us."

It was true. Lorenzo Romano owed his Hollywood career to the Eternity Springs branch of the family.

"I can try, I guess," Gabi said, though her voice was riddled with doubt. "If he's laying low, he has a reason. You know he's never been one to dodge the limelight."

"That's true. It has me a little worried, to be honest. It's why I called in the big guns—you."

Gabi's reply was interrupted by the pounding of boots on the stairs and then the rap of knuckles on his office threshold. "Sorry, boss, but we have a rush. Things are really backing up. Could I get a little help?"

"Sure, I'll be right down." Max grimaced and groaned. "You don't happen to have a disguise tucked away in your backpack, do you? Maybe a wig or a fake mustache?"

"Sorry, left my wig and fake mustache at home today." Gabi unfolded herself from the chair and stood. "But I do have a little time. So I'll sub for you."

"And you'll call our cousin?"

She sighed. "Yes."

"Thank you, Sis. I'll owe you."

"Yes, you absolutely will, and I'll collect. I know just how I'll do it, too."

"How's that?"

A secretive smile formed on her sister's lips. Then, lightly, she said, "You'll find out soon. Maybe Sunday during the family gathering at Aspenglow Place."

"Oh, man. I forgot," Max said, wincing. His maternal great-grandmother, whom the family called Nonnie, had scheduled a long weekend's visit with her granddaughter, their mother, at her home in Eternity Springs. As a result, the four Romano siblings and their families were all invited—actually, commanded—to gather for Sunday dinner at widowed Maggie Romano's B&B. "This Lorenzo business has me completely off my game. I told the Callahans I'd go skiing with them on Sunday."

"You'd better call and cancel. Mom and Nonnie would take turns having your hide if you didn't show for dinner."

"True, that. I'll be there. I wouldn't miss a family dinner with Nonnie for the world." He waited for a beat and added, "I'd be afraid she'd put a curse on me."

"She'd do it, too," Gabi agreed. The Romano siblings shared a smile. "Speaking of Nonnie, maybe you should ask for her help with Lorenzo."

Max considered the idea. A native of Ireland, Nonnie had claimed to be in her eighties for at least the last twenty years. Her insight was credited for everything from the basis of the California branch of the Gallagher family's fortune—she had advocated a stock purchase after a grocery-store conversation with Walt Disney's housekeeper—to the New York branch of the family's success with their pub. And when it came to romance, well, one ignored Nonnie's advice at one's own peril.

"I don't know. Nonnie is impossible to predict. She might not take my side. When is she arriving in town?"

"Tomorrow afternoon, I believe. You know Lorenzo will do whatever Nonnie tells him to do."

"That's true." Lorenzo was a believer, a convert, if you will, to the notion that Nonnie had been gifted with "The Sight." Lorenzo was one of three Romano cousins who'd had their tea leaves read during the festivities surrounding Gabi's wedding, and her predictions led him to move out to LA to pursue an acting career.

Eighteen months later, he was cast in the glitz-and-glamor binge hit *Riviera.* The rest, as they say, was history—a historical pain in Max's ass.

"Tell you what. Call Lorenzo today, and see what he says. If he doesn't cooperate, I'll talk to Nonnie in person tomorrow and try to convince her to drop a GMOAB on our cousin."

"GMOAB?"

"Grandmother of all bombs."

Gabi laughed. "So, what will you do in the meantime? Close the Tipsy Angel? Stay home and play video games?"

"Hey, I'm about to beat the zombie lord. As far as work goes, I'll call Celeste at the Angel's Rest Inn and see if any of her employees can cover for me here at the tasting room for a couple of days. If I have to go out, I'll go with a crowd. I'll wear a hat and sunglasses everywhere."

"Sounds like a plan. I'll phone Lorenzo this afternoon."

"You're awesome, Sis." Max leaned over and kissed her

cheek.

"I know." Gabi blew on her knuckles and polished them against her shoulder. Then she winked and added, "Now, I'd better get out there and help John before he throws in his bar towel and quits."

Max's heart was lighter than it had been in days as he took a seat behind his desk and placed a call to his good friend and Eternity Spring's most beloved citizen, Celeste Blessing.

Once they had exchanged greetings, she said, "This is quite the coincidence. I was just about to call you. I have a favor to ask of a man with muscle, so I thought of you."

"Uh oh. Did I mention I just threw out my back?"

She laughed at his obvious joke. "I need someone strong to put up the decorations tomorrow at Mistletoe Mine. We'll be recreating our Holiday Walking Tour display from this past Christmas, including the Beloved Chamber. Aaron planned to do it for me, but he truly did tweak his back."

"Oh, no. Not too bad, I hope."

"No, he says he's fine, but I can tell he's sore. He'll be fine after a few soaks in our therapeutic hot springs. I'm proposing that he fill in for you at the Tipsy Angel while you're at Mistletoe Mine. As far as that goes, all of the decorations are in storage on site. The work doesn't involve a lot of back and forth, but it is plenty of heavy lifting. Is there any chance you would do this for us?"

"I would love to do heavy lifting at Mistletoe Mine tomorrow. You're the answer to a prayer, Celeste."

"Yes, well, I do try."

So, that was how Max found himself in Mistletoe Mine the following morning armed with keys, a crowbar, plans, and schematics for the electrical parts of the display, along with his toolbox and his work gloves.

Three years ago, when the Eternity Springs Historical Society decided to create a Holiday Walking Tour as a fundraising project, the cavern on Angel's Rest Healing Center and Spa property naturally became the event's highlight stop. The cavern was a magical natural wonder, a labyrinth of chambers filled with glittering stalactites hanging like icicles from the ceilings and majestic stalagmites rising from the floors. Illuminated and decorated for the holiday season, the cavern was a fascinating fairyland that filled visitors with awe. As an added inducement to support the cause, every ticket buyer received a chance to win the Walking Tour's Grand Prize—a night at the Mine Shack, the resort's unique and luxurious apartment, which included a secluded hot springs grotto.

Max spent the day hauling, lifting, and hanging. He decked the halls and jingled the bells. He hammered, screwed, and when the situation warranted, he didn't hesitate to let loose a good solid kick.

Celeste structured her decorations around the theme "Tunnel of Love." The decorations included painted plywood backdrops, artificial trees, music, mannequins, stuffed animals, and angels. Lots and lots and lots of angels. Max hung lights, draped garland, and dangled ornaments. He climbed a ladder about seven thousand times, and he was oh-so-glad to do it.

Long ago, while watching his brother Lucca attempt to deal with the spotlight as a pro basketball player, Max had decided he valued his privacy more than fame or fortune. That's one reason why life in Eternity Springs suited him so well. He really didn't appreciate Lorenzo Romano getting famous and screwing it up for him.

Fangirls gave him the shivers. And not the good kind, either.

CHAPTER 3

CHARMING. THAT WAS THE WORD FOR ETERNITY SPRINGS.

An inch of new snow fell in the valley shortly before Ali's early afternoon arrival, leaving the town picture-perfect and pristine. She'd dawdled on her way into town, stopping to take photographs half a dozen times already.

Aspenglow Place was charming, too. An elegant palette of rose, gold, green, and cream graced the wrap-around porch, gingerbread trim, and window shutters of the Victorian mansion. The innkeeper was charming, too. Maggie Romano welcomed Ali with a friendly smile and gracious hospitality. She wore stylish glasses with cat-eye multicolor frames, gold hoop earrings, and a forest green sweater that matched her eyes atop a pair of black pants. She led Ali up to a cozy, second-floor room that continued the gold and green color palette.

"This is lovely," Ali told her hostess.

"Thank you. We want our guests to be at home while they're here. This weekend will be homey to the rafters. My grandmother is visiting from Denver, and she's brought along a couple of companions, so Aspenglow Place is full. We're all friends and family, though, which I think is perfect for a holiday weekend, don't you?"

"Yes," she replied, meaning it. Being surrounded by coziness and warm family vibes was the perfect distraction from memories of heartbreak past.

Ali unpacked her things, texted Jessica for an ETA, and learned that a plane delay meant her friend wouldn't arrive before dark. Ali would need to visit the photoshoot site this afternoon by herself.

With that task in mind, she searched for the innkeeper and found Maggie in the kitchen tending to her herb garden. Ali explained what she needed regarding the photoshoot.

"You'll want to speak with the owner of Mistletoe Mine, Celeste Blessing," Maggie said. "Let me give you her number."

Ali made the call, and fifteen minutes later, she parked her SUV in a paved lot at Angel's Rest Healing Center and Spa. A woman dressed in a white jacket sporting the resort's logo and driving a glittering gold golf cart pulled up behind Ali's vehicle. "Ms. Lovejoy? I'm Celeste Blessing. Welcome to Angel's Rest."

"Hi. Thank you. Please, call me Ali." Ali snagged her camera bag containing her Hasselblad from the backseat and looped it over her neck so that its weight rested familiarly against her hip. Since she only planned to take a few test photos with natural lighting this afternoon, she didn't bother with any other equipment.

At Celeste's direction, she climbed into the golf cart. They started off across the snow-covered property, Celeste playing tour guide as she drove. She pointed out the resort's main building, the spa, various cabins, and cottages. The afternoon was postcard-perfect, sunny, and the sky above a brilliant blue. Sunlight sparkled like diamonds on the new snow.

"Oh, my, would you look at that?" Celeste removed her foot from the gas pedal, and the cart glided to a stop. "One of the two balloons I've sponsored for this year's festival is floating right over the resort. Oh, I wish I had my camera!"

The hot air balloon was a shimmering gold with the Angel's Rest angel's wings logo in celestial blue. The basket suspended beneath it shimmered an iridescent white.

"Allow me," Ali said with a smile. She stepped from the cart and into a snowdrift, but she hardly noticed the cold. Instead, her attention was focused on framing the photo she wanted. With sure movements developed from long practice, it took her mere seconds to remove her Hasselblad from her bag, lift it to her eye, and snap a few shots.

"Isn't it gorgeous?" Celeste said. "I enjoy all the festivals we host here in Eternity Springs, but the balloon festival is one of my favorites. It's a heavenly feast for the eyes. You should plan to rise early tomorrow and watch it."

"I intend to."

Having gotten the shot she desired, Ali returned to the golf cart. She brushed the powdery snowflakes from her jeans, wishing she'd worn her boots. "I think I got some good ones. I'll send something to you by the end of next week."

"Oh, that is so nice of you. Thank you so much. Be sure to invoice me. You are a professional, after all. And what a good friend you are to Jessica to help her out with this shoot. She told me all about you, and I'm pleased you came to help. We were all devastated that the camera malfunctioned at the big moment."

"It's incredibly kind of you to reset the scene for them."

"I'm just thrilled that our lovebirds can make it back to

Eternity Springs to recreate their important moment. Why, it's a red-letter day for Angel's Rest—a red V for Valentine!"

With that, she suddenly braked the golf cart to a stop. Momentum had Ali jerking forward, then back. "Here we are. This is the side entrance to Mistletoe Mine. This morning, a friend came down to decorate the Tunnel of Love and the Beloved Chamber for tomorrow. He must still be here because the door is open. I'm sure he'll answer any questions you might have."

The Tunnel of Love? Seriously? Jessica never mentioned that.

"Unfortunately, I have an appointment, so I am unable to be your guide. No worries, however. Here's a map."

Celeste handed over a white piece of paper with hand-drawn lines in red ink. In keeping with tomorrow's holiday, she had added plenty of hearts. "I've marked the way for you. It's easy to find. I'm sure you won't have any problem."

"Oh," Ali said, suddenly unsure. Her gaze shifted from the drawing that reminded her of a child's treasure map to the yawning, shadowed opening in the mountain. "Is it, um, safe?"

"No worries. The cavern has been thoroughly mapped. The mine shafts are all closed off."

"Will I be able to see?"

"Oh, yes. The entire thing is wired with electricity. When you're ready to leave, just call the phone number on the map. Someone from the main house will buzz down here and pick you up. Take all the time you need. I want everything to be perfect. There is nothing I love more than smoothing the way for young love."

With a wave and a smile, the older woman took off, leaving Ali alone in front of the yawning hole in the mountain. Trepidation rolled through her. She glanced down at the map. It couldn't be drawn to scale, of course, but it nevertheless appeared to be a long way to the photo site.

What if the electricity failed? This wasn't just an old mine. It was a mountain cave. Animals lived in mountain caves. Mountain lions lived in mountain caves. And mountain bears. Oh my!

She'd just as soon save the horror movies for watching tomorrow night on the laptop, thank you very much.

And yet, Jessica had raved about Celeste Blessing and what an angel she'd been helping Sean set up his original proposal surprise. She could surely trust the woman…right?

"Go boldly," Ali murmured, and she stepped into the cavern.

Immediately, she breathed a sigh of relief. It wasn't so bad. In fact, it wasn't bad at all. The cave was large, and the lights must have been on some sort of motion sensor because they switched on as she stepped inside. Ali was met with Christmas.

A smile broke across her face. How pretty!

Instinct had her lifting her camera to take some shots. Then, in front of one particularly colorful display that looked like a Christmas village made of sugar, she stopped and switched lenses and took some close-up photos.

Ali enjoyed herself. She whistled Rudolf the Red-nosed Reindeer as she wandered slowly along the tunnel, photographing an elf here and an angel there. She could imagine Mistletoe Mine filled with seasonal music and the excited chatter of children's voices. No wonder Jessica had loved this even before the big surprise.

Shortly, Ali arrived at a point where the path split. Since the decorations continued in that direction, her natural inclination guided her to keep right. However, her map clearly showed the Tunnel of Love lay to the left, which made sense because Sean had special arrangements for the engagement.

Ali went left. The cavern narrowed. The tunnel tightened. The air took on a peculiar smell. Not stinky, but different.

Then, suddenly, the temperature changed. It got warm, steamy, almost like a sauna. Then, in front of Ali, the light changed from artificial light to natural light.

Drawn forward by the sunlight, Ali only vaguely noticed the shadowy tunnel off to her right. She sensed…something. Something was different as she entered a larger chamber. It was almost as if—

Ali caught motion off to her right in the periphery of her vision. Turning toward it, she abruptly halted. Her eyes rounded. Her mouth went dry.

Maybe she'd stumbled upon the Tunnel of Love, after all, because the naked male climbing from the steaming pool of water had to be a god. Not a chubby little Valentine's Day Cupid, either. He was all sculpted marble hard body.

This naked god reaching for a fluffy white towel had Eros written all over him.

CHAPTER 4

MAX HEARD A GASP AND A BIT OF A STRANGLED SQUEAK. IT was definitely a very human sound. A feminine sound.

He whipped his head around and absorbed a few things at a glance. Tall. Blonde. Knockout figure. Madonna face.

A camera in her hand.

He dropped his towel. Anger heated his blood as hot as the steaming springs where he'd been soaking his aching muscles. A paparazzo. A peeking, prying, snooping, sneaking picture-peeper.

Who'd just caught "Luscious Lorenzo" buck-ass naked.

Were those dollar signs he saw glittering in her light blue eyes? Bet "Lorenzo Romano" nudes would be worth a pretty penny.

Max stalked toward the woman, his hand outstretched. "Give me the camera. Now."

"Oh. Um. I—" Her eyes round and growing wider with dawning alarm, she backed away. She apparently hadn't noticed the hot springs pool off to the left of the grotto entrance because she continued to retreat. She backed up. She was at the edge of the pool. Her foot reached, found only air, and she teetered.

Max zeroed in on the camera. "Give it—"

She found her balance as Max moved within an arm's length of her.

"—here!" He reached.

She jerked her arm away from his outstretched hand and stepped—

"Ar roof!"

—into the one-hundred-thirty-pound wall that was his Newfie, Barney. She stumbled. And started to tumble.

Max could have made a grab for the woman, but instead, he went for the camera. He managed to snag it by the strap. *Yes!*

Splash.

Serves you right, Shuttersnoop.

Smirking and satisfied, Max scooped up his towel as the intruder came up sputtering. He wrapped the towel around his hips and tucked the ends to secure it before focusing his attention on the camera. He didn't know photography equipment. He seldom took photographs, and when he did, he used his phone. Did cameras still use memory cards?

"Thanks for the help," came a snarky, snippy voice.

"You got all the help you deserved." He glanced her way and, despite his best intentions, did a double-take.

She was in the process of peeling off her leather coat to reveal a blouse—silk, from the looks of it. The color matched her eyes, blue as glacier ice. Soaking wet, the transparent shirt plastered against her like a second skin. Her lacy bra offered minimal concealment, and the stiff peaks of her dusky round nipples drew Max's gaze like magnets.

Though ordinarily a gentleman, this time, Max allowed his eyes to linger. Turnabout and fair play and all of that.

"Ar roof! Ar roof! Ar roof!" Barney nudged up against Max.

Max looked down at his dog, frowned, and muttered softly, "Quit scolding me."

Unfortunately, sound carried in the cave. In the process of spreading her coat on the side of the pool, she glanced at Barney and snapped, "Smart dog."

"Smart mouth," Max fired back, turning his glower toward her. "Here's a little newsflash for you, Shuttersnoop. You picked the wrong Romano to assault. Not only am I not Lorenzo, but my brother is the sheriff in town. You're going to jail."

"What? Wait." She shoved her wet hair back off her face. "I didn't do anything wrong. I have permission to be here."

"Yeah, right." Max studied her camera, located the memory card slot, and slid back the cover.

The peeper screeched. "No! Stop. That's private property."

"They're my privates."

"I didn't take your picture. I swear. I'll show you. Just don't remove the card. You'll destroy the photographs on it. I have new ones I took for Celeste Blessing on the way here this afternoon."

Max's hand stalled. She'd just said the magic Eternity Springs words—Celeste Blessing. He drilled her with a look. "Who are you?"

Standing in waist-high water, she folded her arms over her breasts defensively. "Ali Love—wait a minute. You said your name is Romano?"

"As if this is news."

"As in Maggie Romano? The innkeeper at Aspenglow Place?"

"Lorenzo always said that the paparazzi research everything."

"Lorenzo Romano. You said…whoa." Ali Love-wait-a-minute's chin dropped. "Luscious Lorenzo Romano from *Riviera?* You're him!"

"I didn't say I was Lorenzo. I said I'm *not* Lorenzo! He's *not* in Eternity Springs for the balloon festival. My name is Max. I'm not an actor, and I don't play one on TV. Specifically, not in an Emmy award-winning series that's been ranked number one on Netflix since the latest season dropped. You would be a pitiful paparazzo if your research didn't reveal that Lorenzo has family in Eternity Springs. I'm one of them. His cousin."

"You look just like Lorenzo."

"He looks just like me. I'm older."

"Ah."

"Whoever tipped you off that he was here gave you bad information. How you managed to pull the feathers over Celeste's eyes so that she allowed you into Mistletoe Mine, I'll never know."

"I'm not a paparazzo. I'm a wedding photographer. My college roommate got engaged here on Christmas Eve. The digital photo file got corrupted, so they're recreating the happy event tomorrow. I'm doing the honors so that she gets pictures for her album this time. I just arrived in Eternity Springs today and figured I'd stop by Mistletoe Mine to preview the setting. I'm staying at Aspenglow Place. I assume you're related to Maggie Romano?"

Oh. Max lowered his hand, holding the camera to his side. Her story rang true and fit the facts as he knew them. "She's my mother. What's the groom's name?"

"Is this a test?" When Max shrugged, the intruder rolled

her eyes and answered. "Sean Gallagher. I believe he's related to your family somehow?"

"My mother is a Gallagher." Max admitted, then he asked, "What's your name again?"

"I'm Ali Lovejoy."

"You're from where?"

"Texas. Fort Worth, Texas."

"Long trip."

"Yes, it is."

"So, you really don't have naked pictures of me on your camera?"

"I really don't." A smile tugged at her lips as she added with a touch of humor, "I wasn't quick enough."

Even through the red haze of anger, he'd reacted to her sexiness. Now her teasing grin made her all the more appealing. Against his will and better judgment, attraction wafted through him. His voice naturally turned a little husky as he said, "In that case, maybe I'd better go find my clothes."

"Think you could locate something dry for me to wear while you're at it?" She held up her cell phone. "I'd call Celeste for assistance, but this was in my pocket. It's dead."

Max winced. "Sorry about that. Maybe once it dries out, it'll be okay."

"Maybe," she said, doubt heavy in her tone.

"One of our merchants in town has phones, so we can get you a replacement. In the meantime, I'll look for something dry and warm for you." Max made a quick mental review of the contents of Mistletoe Mine. He could bring her a robe from the Mine Shack suite, but that wouldn't keep her very warm. He could always dash up to the resort store, but it might well be filled with tourists here for the balloon festival. He'd have the Lorenzo factor to face.

Then he remembered the trunks of costumes in the

storage room. Bet one of those red velvet dresses would fit her, and with the faux fur trim, it would be nice and warm. "I'll find something."

"Thank you." She glanced around the cavern in confusion and added, "I don't know how I ended up here. Where am I? I swear I followed Celeste's directions precisely."

Max's mouth twisted in a wry grin. "I'm sure you did. So, you're headed for Beloved Chamber?"

"Yes. That's the place my friend got engaged."

"Either you mixed up your left and right, or Celeste wanted you to visit the grotto. Let me give you a heads up about the Angel's Rest's CEO. Just because Celeste is older, don't make the mistake of thinking that she's a dotty old dear. She's sharp as a tack. You say she asked you to take some photos on the way to the mine this morning?"

"Yes."

"Then she most likely wanted photos of the Mine Shack, too."

"The Mine Shack? I'd have expected something more like 'Hidden Grotto.'"

Max gestured toward a shadowed far wall. "You can't see it from the pool, but there's a door on that back wall. Go through it, and you'll understand. In the meantime, you might as well sink down and enjoy your soak. There's a ledge on the opposite side of the pool that makes an excellent little sitting spot."

"When in Rome," she said with a casual shrug that once again drew his gaze to her breasts.

And here he thought he'd been hot while he soaked in the one-hundred-and-six-degree hot springs.

"Okay, then. I'll be right back." He scooped up his jeans, shirt, and boots and headed into the tunnel with Barney on his heels as usual. After dressing, Max quickly made his way to the storage room where he'd spent so much of his morning. He located the costume trunks and, in short order, found a dress he judged would fit her and a pair of furry white moccasins for her feet.

When he returned to the grotto, he found Ali Lovejoy seated on the sunken ledge in water up to her chin with her head tilted back and her eyes closed. A dreamy smile stretched across her face.

Max was tempted to join her in the pool. However, he doubted she'd appreciate his stripping down again to do so. He hadn't brought a change of clothes with him to Mistletoe Mine this morning. *Guess I could go back and grab that Santa suit from the costume trunk.*

Barney's tags jangled, and Ali opened her eyes and blinked. "You found something?"

"Yes, I believe so. It's a costume from one of the holiday events here at Mistletoe Mine. I think it'll fit you okay, and it should keep you warm until we can get you back to Aspenglow Place."

"Thank you, although I'll admit I'm in no rush to get dry. This is the most fabulous hot springs ever. It's the first one I've ever been around that doesn't stink like rotten eggs."

"That's sulfur. You don't get sulfur here. Too demonic." He grinned crookedly as he added, "Our resident angel Celeste wouldn't hear of it."

"She's very good with branding, isn't she? Lots of angel wings."

"They're everywhere."

"Does she add something to the water? These springs smell like mint. I've never heard of hot springs that smell like mint. Mint isn't a mineral."

"Yeah, well, at Christmastime, it smells like cinnamon in here."

"You're kidding." When Max shook his head, she asked, "But this is a real cavern. Inside a real mountain. I didn't take a wrong turn into Disneyland, did I? Or tumble into Wonderland?"

"You're in Eternity Springs, Colorado, Ms. Lovejoy."

"Ali," she hastened to say. "Call me Ali."

"I'm Max, and consider this fair warning. Here in Eternity Springs, the extraordinary sometimes seems downright run-of-the-mill. A minty hot spring is pretty par for the course."

"Well, I love it. I can just feel the stiffness from traveling and the stress seeping away. It's almost worth the price of a new phone. I'm overdue on an upgrade anyway."

Max carried the dress and shoes to the bench near the wall where Celeste kept a basket of towels. "If you want to soak a little longer, no need to rush. I still have some work to do setting up the scene for your photographs. Want me to come back in, say, half an hour? Or I could tell you how to find me. You only took one wrong turn."

"Why don't you tell me how to find you, but if I don't show up in half an hour, you can come looking for me?"

"Sounds like a plan." Max gave her precise and detailed instructions on how to find Mistletoe Mine's Beloved Chamber. Then, picking up his damp towel from where he'd dropped it, he gestured toward a doorway that blended in with the surrounding walls, making it virtually hidden. "The Mine Shack is through there. If you want to shower before you dress, make yourself at home. Celeste won't mind. The door to the bathroom is the blue one. The cream-colored door leads to the Mine Shack's main entrance. We entered the grotto by the back way."

"There's a shower here, too?"

Max nodded. "Yes, and it's some shower. I'm sure you'll

want to get a shot or two of it while you are snapping photos for Celeste. So, anything else before I go?"

"I don't believe so."

"All right, then. I'll see you in half an hour." Max turned to leave, determined to steer his mind away from devilish fantasies about Ali Lovejoy standing naked beneath the Mine Shack's waterfall shower and turn his attention toward the angelic.

CHAPTER 5

"RED AND WHITE," ALI MUTTERED. SCOWLING, SHE WRAPPED the luxurious Turkish cotton bath sheet around her torso. She eyed the garment Max Romano had left for her to wear. Ali didn't wear red and white or pink and white during February. How fitting that he'd bring her Valentine's colors to wear.

But then she picked up the folded fabric and took a good look at it. "Oh wow."

It was a heavy dress made from red velvet, red silk charmeuse, and trimmed with soft white fur. As Ali unfolded it, she spied red sequins. Then something furry and white dropped from within its pleats.

"Eek!" She squealed as it fell at her feet.

Immediately, she realized the thing wasn't alive, thank goodness. "A muff. It's a muff."

The girl who'd loved to play dress-up while growing up was delighted.

Understanding dawned. And this was a costume. As she gave it a thorough look, delight spread through her. This was one of the gowns from the final scene in *White Christmas*—Ali's all-time favorite Christmas movie. She watched it every year on Thanksgiving weekend to start her holidays off right. Was it Rosemary Clooney's dress or Vera-Ellen's?

She held it by the shoulders. It had a turtleneck and belted waist. It was Vera-Ellen's. "Gorgeous. It's gorgeous."

Ali decided that she didn't dare wear a costume of this beauty without showering first.

Gathering up the items Max had left for her, she reflected on the crazy turn this day had taken. First meeting a naked and angry Adonis in the middle of a mountain, and now the opportunity to wear a quality reproduction of one of her favorite costumes of all time—forget her aversion to wearing Valentine's colors in February. If ever there was a time for an exception, it was now.

She carried the costume toward the hidden door. A short tunnel led to another entrance, green with a white plaque that read The Mine Shack. Ali opened the door, and her eyes went wide.

It was like stepping into a combination theme park and Four Season's Hotel. A king-sized bed sat atop a plush Turkish rug and dominated the space. An overstuffed chair and ottoman positioned in front of a fireplace provided a perfect place to read or simply watch the flames from the gas logs dance. Opposite the bed stood a cabinet containing a small refrigerator, a coffee maker, snacks, and a fully stocked bar.

Ali scanned a framed, handwritten letter from Celeste Blessing placed on the nightstand beside the bed. It welcomed VIP visitors to Angel's Rest's Mine Shack—the most private accommodations in Eternity Springs.

Ali wondered how much a night in the Mine Shack set a person back. A pretty penny, she'd bet. But, maybe someday, she would build her business to such lofty heights that she'd have the budget for a weekend at the Mine Shaft. Or, perhaps she could take some totally awesome photographs today and do a little bartering with the innkeeper.

Maybe that's why Celeste sent her in the wrong direction in the first place.

Ali opened the blue door to the bathroom and again did a complete stop. Could the space be any more luxurious? A soaking tub with a rainfall faucet from the roof above and a fireplace. The shower was separate, a huge walk-in. Max was right. This was some shower. A vanity with lights and every sort of grooming product imaginable sat against one wall. Hmm. If she hurried through her shower, maybe she could dry her underwear with the hairdryer.

A wooden wardrobe stood next to the vanity. Ali opened it in search of a hanger for the velvet dress. She stopped. Men's clothing hung inside, and an expensive leather suitcase sat in the wardrobe's base.

Huh. Suspicion fluttered through Ali's mind. Wait a minute. Could he be lying to her? What if this whole "Max" business was a lie? What if he really was Lorenzo Romano? He did look *exactly* like the television star.

Well, it was the middle of February, after all. Almost Valentine's Day, when the men in her life proved themselves as liars and cheaters and scumbags.

"Now there's a cynical hot take," she observed, chastising herself. She didn't believe the theory. It would be too easy to check. However, it did appear that the Mine Shack already had a guest, and she was trespassing.

But the bathroom had a door that locked, and since she'd already committed the sin, she might as well enjoy it. Besides, she'd be in and out quick as a minute.

Quick as a minute stretched to almost ten. The selection of handmade soaps available in the shower added time because Ali took that long to choose. The scent and the luxurious lather seduced her into trying the shampoo and conditioner. Loved them, too! She'd have to pay a visit to Heavenscents while she was in Eternity Springs.

Since she'd already blown her quick-as-a-minute plan, she decided to test the steam shower setting. More fabulousness. When she finally dragged herself from the shower and reached for one of the fluffy white bath sheets, Ali had concluded that Celeste Blessing's choice of angel's wings for her resort logo fit the bill. The Mine Shack was a little slice of heaven.

She sat at the vanity, dried and styled her hair, and took advantage of the Angel's Rest Spa and Salon makeup sampler. Drying her lacy undergarments took no time at all, and by the time she wrangled the zipper of the velvet dress, she could all but hear the violins playing.

Wait a minute. Ali *did* hear violins playing, something slow and soft and romantic.

She opened the bathroom door to find Max stretched out on the bed, his back propped up against pillows, his elbows extended with his fingers laced behind his head. His gaze swept her from head to toe. "Well, this is a surprise. I expected naked."

"Excuse me?"

"Instead, you're covered from head to toe. Nice twist. Unusual. I guess you're shooting for being a Valentine gift all ready for me to unwrap? Damned if I'm not tempted. You make a gorgeous package. Unfortunately, I'm expecting a visitor at any moment. Family, otherwise I'd hang out the 'Do Not Disturb' sign."

"Max," she began, confused, and then it hit her. This wasn't Max. He wore a white shirt and jeans. Max's shirt was green. "You're not Max."

"Max?" Interest lit his eyes. He swung his legs off +the

bed and stood. "You were expecting Max? Isn't that interesting." He flashed her a dazzling smile. "What's your name?"

Instinctively, she answered. "Ali."

"Hello, beautiful Ali. You know, I was going to guess Judy. Judy Haynes. Do you dance, Ali?"

Dance? Still confused. "Um, yes. Why do—?"

"Alexa, play 'The Best Things Happen While You're Dancing.'"

Then before she realized what was happening, music began to play. He took her in his arms and began to dance. Then he started singing to her.

OMG.

She was dancing with Lorenzo Romano.

Lorenzo Romano was singing to her! One of the songs right out of *White Christmas.*

Double OMG.

Too bad it's not Max.

From the doorway came an excellent Humphrey Bogart impression. "Of all the closed silver mines in all the small towns in all the world, he has to invade mine."

CHAPTER 6

MAX WAS STEAMING MAD, SO HIS TONE WAS AS COLD AS THE summit of Sinner's Prayer Pass on Valentine's Day. Nevertheless, he added some warmth to the smile he gave Ali. "Ali? Are you ready to go and finish our project?"

She stepped away from Lorenzo, then glanced at the man whom Max pointedly ignored. "Um…sure."

"Aren't you going to say hello, Max?" Lorenzo asked.

"I'm following your lead and pretending you're not here."

His cousin's tone bristled. "What do you mean by that?"

"You've been here at least a week, I'll bet, haven't you? Probably more like ten days. That's when my world started going to hell."

"Look, I heard you've had some issues. I spoke to Gabi. In fact, she's on her way here now. But listen, Max, there's something you don't know. It wasn't my idea to come here. I was just following orders."

Max snorted. "Right. Let me guess. Your trainer wanted you to run mountain trails? Your aesthetician decided that mountain air makes your pores smaller? No, what am I thinking? Obviously, your agent sent you to Eternity Springs because, of course, money is involved."

The television star's expression grew sulky. "You are such an ass, Max. I'll have you know I'm here at the special request of Celeste Blessing."

Max folded his arms. Okay, he could buy that. She could be setting up some special Valentine's Day surprise for one of her guests at Angel's Rest.

Except, she hadn't said anything about Lorenzo to him yesterday or today. Considering the family connection between him and Lorenzo and the problems his cousin's presence in town had caused him, that wasn't like her.

Lorenzo continued. "It's part of a special surprise for your mother."

"Mom?"

"Yes! Celeste called me a month ago and gave me explicit instructions. I needed to be in Eternity Springs from February fourth through the fifteenth. I canceled an appearance on *Saturday Night Live* to be here, so you need to get off my back."

"What surprise? The family hasn't planned any surprise."

"Maybe you're part of it."

"That doesn't make any sense." Except, maybe it did make some sense. Suddenly, puzzle pieces began to fit together. Celeste had directed Ali to the Mine Shack, not the Beloved Chamber, where the photos were to be shot. She'd also encouraged Max to take advantage of the Mine Shack's hot springs when he'd finished moving the heavy crates. In Eternity Springs, Celeste Blessing was known for her wisdom, kindness, business acumen, and her tendency to play Cupid with couples in town. She'd never turned her attention Max's way, so he'd never worried about the matchmaking part of her personality.

That could have changed.

Celeste had joined the Romano family for dessert on Thanksgiving Day. She'd been present when, on an Italian cream cake high, Max had allowed his great-grandmother to cajole him into letting her read his tea leaves. It was her special recipe, after all. How could he have refused?

Oh, holy oolong. Max dragged his hand down his jawline and across his mouth. Had Celeste sent Ali Lovejoy on a wild Romano chase?

Max was a pragmatic man. He'd witnessed enough meddling and miracles in Eternity Springs to know that Celeste was gonna Celeste. No sense trying to stop her. He might as well sit back and enjoy the ride. She might encourage love along, but in the end, people still make their own decisions.

And as far as Nonnie's reading went, well, Fate was gonna Fate, too. No sense worrying about that, either.

Max had nothing against romance. Truth be told, he envied his siblings' happy marriages. Max wanted children. He simply hadn't found the woman with whom he wanted to spend the rest of his life. He'd thought he'd come close a time or two, but when he got married, he wanted it to be forever. No divorce, no do-overs. So, he was taking his time. Too much time, according to his mother.

But a surprise for his mother that he knew nothing about? And why bring Lorenzo into it? That made no sense. He wasn't quite sure what to think at this point.

Still, the idea of Celeste Blessing and his great-grandmother teamed up together made the hair on the back of his neck rise.

Having grown impatient with Max's silence, Lorenzo rolled his eyes dramatically and sighed. He turned to Ali and gave a slight bow. "I am Lorenzo Romano, and as you have undoubtedly surmised, I am this blackguard's cousin."

"Blackguard," Max repeated with a snort of disgust. "He's been wearing people out with that term ever since he played a pirate captain in a pilot for a series that didn't get picked up. We all give thanks for that blessing."

Ignoring Max, Lorenzo continued. "I apologize for mistaking you for a trespasser. I hope you'll allow me the opportunity to make it right. Perhaps dinner tomorrow night?"

"Tomorrow is Valentine's Day," Max pointed out. "You won't be able to get a table anywhere in town. Shoot, in a hundred miles of town."

"I'm Lorenzo Romano. I can get a table wherever I want, whenever I want."

Suddenly, Max had had enough. Feeling territorial where Ali was concerned, whether he had a right to do so or not, he crossed the room and took her hand. "We already have plans, and we've wasted enough time talking to you. Barney, heel."

As Max tugged Ali toward the grotto, Lorenzo called a parting shot. "If your plans change, Ali, let me know. You look beautiful in red, by the way. It's definitely your color."

"Blackguard," Max muttered and slammed the door behind them as they entered the grotto.

Laughing softly, Ali gestured toward her camera bag, which she'd left beside the pile of towels. Then, when he veered toward it, she asked, "Do you have a little pirate in you, too, Max?"

"Arrrr. I'd like to keelhaul Lorenzo."

That made her laugh out loud. "And here I imagined you as a different sort of captain entirely."

"A captain?" he repeated as he led her away from the

grotto through the tunnel that would take them to the Beloved Chamber.

"Yes. Do you sing?"

"Do I sing? Why do you ask? You've lost me."

"Well, join the crowd." Ali frowned as the tunnel widened and split into three branches. "This is totally not the way Celeste's map told me to go."

"Celeste usually has her reasons for doing whatever she does. So what's this about a captain?"

"Bing Crosby. He was an Army captain in *White Christmas.* Although, I half expected you to greet me in a Santa suit to match my dress."

"Ah." Max nodded. "Yes, there is a matching Santa suit in the costume trunk, but I draw the line at sequins, Ali. Just so you know."

"I'll keep that in mind. So, what about the singing?"

"I'm no Bing, but I can carry a tune as good as Lorenzo. See the red lights up ahead? That's where we join the decorated section of the walking tour. It's about midway between the Mistletoe Mine entrance and the Beloved Chamber, where Sean proposed to your friend. Her name is Jessica, right?"

"Right."

"As an FYI, the theme of this year's walking tour was 'Our Treasures.' It highlighted the history of Eternity Springs, along with family and friendship. Celeste is a decorating fiend, and she's partial to angels."

"I noticed that on my way in. So, you set up all these decorations today? No wonder you wanted to soak in the hot springs."

"Unfortunately, I'm not entirely finished. I still have two naked Christmas trees that need ornaments. It won't take long to do, but after all the heavy lifting, Barney and I decided we needed a little break."

"Speaking of Barney…" Ali gestured toward his dog, who had turned the opposite direction from where they were headed.

"He's fine. He'll go outside when he needs to, and he has a bowl of water and a bed in the storeroom. Barney's a good dog—when he's not knocking beautiful women off their feet."

She darted him a shy smile that acknowledged the compliment, then returned her attention to the decorations. "I should have asked Jessica what she and Sean are wearing. There isn't a lot of color here."

True. Everything was either gold, silver, or white. Max explained, "It's different inside. The Beloved Chamber has a particular stalactite that lends itself to, well, you'll see."

Pausing outside the entrance to their destination, Max's gaze swept over Ali once more. The costume might have been designed for *White Christmas,* but it couldn't suit this time, this place, or this woman more perfectly.

A Valentine all wrapped up in red and white. Was she destined to be his Beloved?

Did Max honestly believe in tea leaves and angels?

Time would tell.

CHAPTER 7

"HERE WE ARE," MAX SAID. HE WAVED HER FORWARD, saying, "After you, Shutterbug. Ladies first."

Ali walked inside and drew in a wondering breath. The stalactite was shaped like a heart, not a human heart like at the famous Timpanogos Cave National Monument in Utah, but a classic Valentine heart. This time, the chamber was decorated in shadow and lights—red and white hearts and angels—Cupids.

The only wood in this chamber was a graceful pedestal set off to one side. It held an old, worn Bible bound in red leather, turned to the Book of John. A spotlight highlighted the passage 3:16. Ali read aloud, "For God so loved the world…."

"That's the family bible from one of Eternity Springs' founding families. Daniel Murphy is the spelunker who gave Beloved its name, based on that passage."

"This is fabulous. Jessica attempted to describe this to me, but her words didn't do it justice."

"Come, stand over here. You'll want to see Beloved from this perspective to frame your shots."

Max indicated a spot where the stalactite hung, centered between two artificial Christmas trees. They currently had lights but no ornaments. The naked ones to which he'd referred, she deduced.

"I'm told Sean proposed to Jessica right over there. Celeste had me put the trees back up to recreate the moment, though the ornaments are more in keeping with Valentine's Day this time around. Do you think it'll look okay for the shoot?"

Ali studied the spot with a photographer's eye. "Perfect."

"You'll want to get a wide view. Look up."

Ali did, and then she laughed. "I take it that's mistletoe? Being held by a Cupid?"

"Leave it to Celeste Blessing to cram Christmas and Valentine's Day together. Can it possibly get hokier than this, do you think?"

"Probably, but it would take some effort."

"That said, you can't argue with success. Angel's Rest doesn't advertise the Beloved Chamber. It's all word-of-mouth, and Celeste is very particular about who is allowed access to this part of Mistletoe Mine. Despite those restrictions, she told me they had eight marriage proposals here this year."

"This is the place for it," she observed, gazing around. "I don't believe I've ever seen so many hearts."

"Celeste is nothing if not enthusiastic when it comes to romance. And angels. And Christmas. And friends. And advice. She's a lot like my great-grandmother."

He paused and studied the stalactite, then reflected aloud, "They're wise women. Both of them."

Ali waited for Max to say more, but she pivoted to her reason for being here when he remained silent and thoughtful.

In a crisp, professional tone, she asked, "Can I assume that the lighting remains constant in Beloved Chamber?"

He gave his head a shake as though shrugging off a disturbing thought. "Yes, but everything is adjustable. Plus, I brought a couple of studio lights from the storage room if you want to use them."

"Fabulous."

He helped her set them up, and while she busied herself testing settings with lights and camera, he opened one of two plastic tubs filled with tree trimming supplies. Ali couldn't resist sneaking a couple of shots of Max as he strung garland and hung ornaments on one of the naked Christmas trees. He was so darned sexy dressed in his jeans and green flannel shirt. However, the memory of his Eros attire lay tucked away, ready to be savored like a chocolate-covered caramel.

She couldn't say precisely why, but she would have liked to have seen him in the Santa suit that matched her dress. Or maybe just the pointed Santa hat with the pompom. And nothing else. That was easy enough to imagine.

She'd add that one to her box of fantasy chocolates.

Ali grinned at herself and started humming, "White Christmas." Halfway through the relatively short song, Max shocked her by joining in—singing the lyrics!

Maybe not Bing, but still a smooth, rich baritone, like a maple nut buttercream that made her mouth water.

Okay, enough. This wasn't like her. Must be the influence of all the hearts and little fat angels. *Step away from the chocolates. Keep your mind on Christmas!*

As the final bars of the tune faded, she said, "*White Christmas* is my favorite holiday movie. The title song is my favorite holiday song."

"Plot was cheesy, but the music and costumes were great. The women in my family made us watch it every year. I didn't mind. Both ladies were hot, but I was Team Judy. Betty had more curves, but Judy's legs…." He sighed longingly and made Ali laugh.

"You did me a real solid by choosing Vera-Ellen's gown for me to wear."

"Because it's warm and comfortable or because you're not a Rosemary Clooney fan?"

"Neither. I'm not a fan of Valentine's Day. All the red and white and hearts and Cupids are overwhelming for me. But if I focus on the Christmas trees and this dress, which clearly shouts Christmas, I can block out the Valentine's element."

"What do you have against Cupid?"

"It's a long story and a long-term policy. Suffice to say, I don't buy into the crass commercial-created frenzy surrounding February fourteenth."

"Huh." Max looped a red glass heart around an artificial tree branch, then turned to study her. He folded his arms and stared.

Ali grew defensive, and her chin came up. "What?"

"It's just that everything has become clear to me now," he replied, his tone serious and sincere. "There's only one thing to do. You are going to have to marry me."

Following a moment of shock, she burst out laughing. His answering grin warmed her to her fuzzy white moccasins. "I take it you're not a Valentine's Day fan either?"

"Nope. I despise the Day of Hearts." He returned his attention to his decorating task. He still had about one-third of the first tree and the entire second tree left to decorate.

"Any particular reason?"

"A whole list of them. The cost of a date triples on February fourteenth. Restaurants are packed. You have to make reservations weeks in advance, and the menus are limited and expensive. If you're in a new relationship, it's almost impossible to know the expected scale. If you're in a long-term relationship, you have to top what you did the previous year. And then there are the stupid nonstop radio commercials! Teddy bears and pajamas and chocolate-covered fruit. One-eight-hundred shut the hell up!"

"Exactly! That's exactly right." Ali beamed at him. "Okay. Yes, I'll marry you. We are obviously made for each other."

"Excellent. My mother will be so relieved. I'm the last of her chicks to tie the knot. She worries about me. How does next Tuesday sound?"

"Hmm." Ali adjusted the position of one of the studio lights. "Tuesday isn't good. I'm getting highlights in my hair."

"You're not a natural blonde?"

"That's a personal question."

"We're getting married. A husband needs to know such things."

"No, he doesn't."

"Okay, how about Thursday?"

She clicked her tongue, then checked her light meter. "Not good, either. I have Stars tickets."

"Dallas Stars?"

"Yes."

"Wait a minute." In the process of hanging a red sequined heart on the tree, he halted and turned to look at her in mock shock. "You'd skip our wedding to watch a hockey game?"

"What can I say? I'm a fan."

"You are an interesting woman, Ali Lovejoy."

"Thank you. That's a nice compliment." She waited for a beat, then added, "I'm free on Monday."

"Mm..." He winced and shook his head. "Can't do it. Barney has an appointment at the groomers."

"Well, shoot. I guess we're not meant to be, after all." She adjusted the light and took another reading, then nodded. "This is good. I'm done here. Need some help?"

"Please." He gestured to the tub filled with cupids and hearts.

She crossed the room and stood over the plastic bin, debating her choices. She did hope Jessica was wearing red. She often did. The visual for this photo indeed would be stunning.

Max interrupted her musing. "I suppose you caught my comment to my cousin about the two of us having Valentine's Day plans?"

She chose a red heart and darted him a glance. "Now that you mention it, yes. Yes, I did."

"I appreciate you not calling me out on it."

Ali hung the ornament on the green artificial Douglas fir bough. "It *was* presumptuous of you. I mean, a date with a television star on Valentine's Day? That could be a pretty big scoreboard in certain circles."

He tilted his head and studied her. "Do you run in certain circles?"

"Nah." She reached for a Cupid. "I pretty much travel in squares."

"I knew I liked you."

Ali wanted to preen. She hadn't flirted like this with a hot guy in a very long time, and it did her ego good.

"So, do you want to make an honest man out of me and hang with me some tomorrow?"

Ali hesitated. Hang out? On Valentine's Day?

Hanging out was not a date. Hanging out covered lots of things that wouldn't conflict with horror flicks on her laptop. "What are you thinking?"

"Well, your photoshoot is tomorrow afternoon, correct?"

"Early afternoon, yes."

"There's a balloon festival in town. It's awesome to watch if you're inclined to get up early. A friend of mine would be happy to take us up if you'd like to ride along. Or if hot air balloons aren't your thing, you could join me at the school gymnasium and help decorate for tomorrow night's sweetheart dance. I'm going there after the balloon festival."

Ali couldn't hide her surprise. "It occurs to me that I haven't asked what you do for a living. Are you an interior designer, Max?"

The question obviously startled him. "What? No! I make beer! I own a microbrewery."

"Really? That sounds interesting."

"It is. I'm good at it. I own the Tipsy Angel label."

She pictured a logo with a golden-haired angel wearing a crooked halo and a happy smile. "I've had that beer at Sean's house. The Christmas ale this year was exceptional."

"Thank you."

"So you just decorate for fun?"

He gave her a droll look. "This is an unusual weekend. I'm doing favors for friends—and hiding from Lorenzo's fan club."

"Ah. I see. Well, I'd love to hang out with you tomorrow. I'd planned to attend the balloon festival, and I'd love to go for a ride in one. I've never done that. As far as decorating the gym goes, can we play that by ear? It may be one Cupid too many for me."

"Fair enough. Completely understandable." He placed one final ornament on the tree he was decorating, then moved to help with hers. After he hung the second ornament, he asked, "So, are you seeing anyone back home? I'm not stepping on any toes, am I?"

She frowned at him. "You invited me to hang out

together. That's not toe-steppable."

"Technically, that's true. I just like a defined dance floor."

Ali shrugged. "Well, metaphors aside, I'm capital S single. I have been since February fifteenth of last year."

"A really bad Valentine's Day?"

"Par for my course."

He waited, watching her expectantly. Ali didn't mind sharing the story. It wasn't her sin, after all. "We'd been together for three years, living together for one, and our wedding was set for June fifth. Then, last year on February thirteenth, I discovered a traditional Valentine's stash in the garden shed. Everything but the flowers—a teddy bear, lingerie, perfume, diamond earrings, and a romantic card."

"That's some stash."

"Overkill, don't you think?" Max shrugged, and Ali continued her explanation. "Our rules were no cards—seriously, even a simple card can cost eight dollars now, it's ridiculous—and one small gift. I love chocolates. I'm always happy with a box of chocolates. There weren't any chocolates in his stash."

"So, a red flag."

"Yep, but one I tried to ignore. I didn't want to believe it. Anyway, he went off to work that morning without giving me a gift. Flowers never arrived at the office. That evening, we ordered out like we'd planned. He presented nothing with the pizza. I told myself, okay, he'll shower me with gifts after sex. Instead, he turned over and started to snore. So, I got out of bed and checked his hiding place. Empty as his lying, cheating heart."

"What did you do?"

"Well, he's an attorney, and he'd invested in my business, so I knew I needed to be careful. I wanted to consult my own attorney before I did anything." She paused a moment, flicked a heart ornament with her finger, and then added with a dramatically innocent and exaggerated Texas drawl, "It was terrible luck that I turned the steering wheel so sharply while backing out of the garage. I somehow managed to hook his golf bag with my bumper and drag it halfway down the street before I realized it."

"Ouch."

Ali clucked her tongue. "Turns out his new honey had gifted him with a new driver for Valentine's Day."

"Karma is a witch," Max said solemnly.

"She truly is." Ali eyed the tree. Three, maybe four more ornaments, and they'd be done, she decided. "So back to the metaphors. Since I waved around all my dirty laundry, how about you take the dance floor? Your turn."

"I've already had a turn. You've seen me naked. What more can I possibly reveal?"

"You tell me."

"Okay, I don't mix my metaphors or cheat on my lovers. I'm free to hang out to my heart's content." He scooped up three more ornaments from the tub and quickly hung them on the tree. Stepping back, he gave both trees a quick once over. "I think that's good, don't you?"

"You don't have toppers?"

"Forgot!" He snapped his fingers. "Celeste keeps the toppers separate. A local glass artist made them, and they're a bit of a treasure. They're in the Mistletoe Mine office. Want to test the sound system for me while I run to get them? That's the final thing on the agenda."

"Sure. How do I do it?"

"There's a control panel about ten feet to the right of the door at waist level. See it?" He pointed toward the panel.

"Yes." Ali moved toward it.

"There's a switch at the top for light. I'll be back in a

few."

"All right."

Ali couldn't get the sound system to work. She fiddled with the switches and dials without success until Max returned to the room carrying two small boxes. "No luck?"

"No," she replied, accepting the box he handed to her.

"I was afraid of that. Celeste told me it's been finicky."

"We don't necessarily need it for the photographs."

"You'll want to pipe in a little music for atmosphere, believe me. Also, Celeste is a perfectionist when it comes to her projects. If I can't get the sound to work, I'll tell her she needs to send her electrician."

Ali forgot about the electrical problems when she removed the box lid to reveal an actual work of art nestled in blue velvet. "Oh, wow." She carefully lifted the glass angel holding a red crystal heart fixed atop a glittering silver spiral cone from the box. As she held it to the light, color danced and the piece came to life. Her lips spread in a slow smile. "It's absolutely gorgeous."

Max spoke in a husky voice. "Yeah. Definitely."

Ali darted a glance his way, and the air in Beloved Chamber suddenly grew heavier, hotter. Ali swallowed hard.

She recalled how he'd looked climbing out of the hot springs pool. Mouth-wateringly delicious.

Clearing her throat, she gave her head a shake and carried the topper over to the tree she'd been decorating. Max followed with the second box, which held a matching topper. While he crowned the first tree, she went up on her tiptoes and reached. She felt herself teetering. She fought for balance.

Hello! Déjà vu all over again. Thank goodness Barney wasn't around this time. She absolutely could not drop this work of art!

Then Max's arm slid around her waist. He pulled her against him, steadying her. "Careful there," came that delicious baritone against her ear. "Here. Let me help."

He felt sturdy as the mountain and hot as the springs. The shiver that ran up Ali's spine had nothing to do with the temperature of the room. Then he fitted both hands around her waist and lifted her.

"There you go," he murmured, his voice deeper and a little husky.

"Th-th-thanks." With trembling hands, she topped the tree. Ever so carefully, one by one, she released her fingers from the glass treasure. *Whew.*

Continuing to hold her, Max stepped away from the trees. Then, in the quiet of the cavern, she heard him draw a deep breath. "You smell like apple pie."

Her nerves hadn't calmed the least little bit. If anything, she'd grown more agitated. "It's the Heavenscents shampoo. And soap. Body lotion. I used everything."

"Cinnamon and spice and everything nice." Holding her against him, he lowered her slowly to her feet. "I didn't do this on purpose, I promise, but fair warning, Ali. Fate is a powerful force. Look where we are."

As her head fell back and her face lifted, his hands skimmed down to her hips. Even as she spied and identified the mistletoe, he was turning her around. "I can't resist dessert."

Max Romano's lips met Ali's in a kiss that quickly turned as steamy as the Mine Shack grotto.

Her pulse sped. Her blood hummed. Her arms crept up and circled Max's neck as yearning swept through her. It had been a year since she'd been kissed.

And she'd never been kissed by a man like Max.

She wanted to press herself against him, to experience the

sensation of that large, hard body molded to hers. She wanted to lose herself in the magic of this chamber, the mystery of this man, and the marvel of the mouth moving hot and mercilessly against hers. Was her reaction this strong because she hadn't been kissed so long? Or because he could have modeled for Michelangelo's *David*?

No, she didn't think so. She thought it was the man. This man. Max. He even had a Roman name. She would have giggled if she had the extra breath.

He captured her head in his hands, sinking his fingers into her hair, drinking from her lips like he was drowning. The intensity of his reaction sent a giddy sense of power sizzling through her.

Oh, how Ali had missed this—the passion, the sharing, the excitement. When he muttered words against her mouth, she made out only one. It sounded like…destiny.

Destiny?

Suddenly, music blared from the sound system and broke them apart. For a long moment, they stood staring into one another's eyes. Then, it slowly dawned upon Ali that the song playing wasn't a Christmas carol. It wasn't "White Christmas" or "Jingle Bells" or "Silent Night." It wasn't "Santa Baby" or "Rudolph the Red-Nosed Reindeer." .

No, instead "Going to the Chapel" was blasting from the sound system.

Ali blinked. Her mouth gaped. This was all a little too much.

Breathing heavily, Max raked his fingers through his thick, black hair and said the strangest thing. "I give up, Nonnie."

"What?"

"Never mind." He shook his head. "Ali, will you go to dinner with me tomorrow night?"

CHAPTER 8

She said no.

Max suspected that the primary reason why Ali refused his dinner invitation had been bad timing. The intensity of the kiss they'd exchanged had spooked her. Of course, it hadn't helped anything that he'd gone and mumbled about Gallagher family lore.

Truth be told, once they'd exited the Beloved Chamber and Mistletoe Mine and emerged into the light of day, he'd been glad she'd turned him down. He'd been a little too caught up in the blazing heat of her kiss and the woo-woo aura of the moment. Max might believe there was something to Nonnie and her tea leaves, but that didn't mean it all had to move at warp speed. Besides, he'd still see her first thing in the morning. Their balloon festival date was still on. After that, well, nothing was set in stone.

Although, technically speaking, stalactites were stone. Beloved was a stone. Was Ali Lovejoy destined to be his beloved?

Since he couldn't answer that question immediately, he'd turned his attention to the one posed by his cousin's presence at the Mine Shack. He'd called a sibling meeting for that evening. He was serving spaghetti to the Romano masses at his home out at Hummingbird Lake.

A knock on the door interrupted the conversation. It signaled the arrival of the first group of family members, Max's younger brother Lucca and his wife and children. His elder brother Zach and his wife and kids arrived a few minutes later. Finally, his sister and her husband, Flynn Brogan, completed the guest list.

Max waited until everyone's plates were filled to address the subject that had been burning in his belly all afternoon. Casually, he asked, "So, Gabriella, care to share with the class what mischief you and Celeste are cooking up with Lorenzo?"

Gabi dropped her fork. A flush of guilt stained her cheeks.

Flynn said, "Cat's out of the bag, love. Might as well go ahead and tell them."

Gabi drew in a deep breath, then met Max's gaze. "I'm so sorry, Max. I never dreamed I would cause this much trouble."

The explanation gave the family much to discuss, and the conversation went on for some time. Max soon realized that Gabi failed to understand that she, too, was a pawn in the machinations of others. However, he decided to keep that particular truth to himself for the time being. Telling it would only prolong the evening. His sister was visibly exhausted, and he had an early morning. Besides, he figured matters would be clearer by tomorrow night, right? When Valentine's Day was done?

The following morning, he arrived at Aspenglow Place at the pre-arranged five a.m. to find an excited Ali ready and waiting with fresh hot coffee in the kitchen.

"I trust Sean and Jessica made it safe and sound?"

"Yes, but not until almost ten o'clock. They were both exhausted. I told them I had plans to watch the balloons take off, so they should sleep in this morning. I want them to be fresh for the photos."

They spoke about their respective Friday evenings during the drive out to Hummingbird Lake. Almost a hundred hot air balloons covered the frozen surface in various stages of fill in preparation for the morning's mass ascension, and the scene was a sea of brilliant color. Having recently done a community-related favor for the town's sheriff, his brother Zach, Max had wrangled a prime festival parking space.

Ali bubbled like champagne as they walked among the balloonists, visiting and taking photographs. She giggled like an eight-year-old at the Macy's Thanksgiving parade when she caught sight of Celeste's new balloon for this year. In addition to Angel's Rest's traditionally shaped balloon, Celeste had added a specialty shape that came complete with angel wings this year.

The balloons launched beginning at sunrise in two waves. Max found the professional-at-work Ali fascinating. She definitely had an artist's eye.

They hitched a ride in a balloon and spent two hours sailing above Eternity Springs and the surrounding valley. By the time they landed, and she declared she'd taken all the photos she wished, Max was enchanted. He didn't want their time together to end.

Apparently, neither did she. Because before Max could figure a way to extend their morning, she turned to him and asked, "Is that gym decorating invitation still open?"

"It is. We can use all the help we can get. Have you decided to brave the hearts and flowers, after all?"

"I think it might be good for me. Maybe all the Cupids yesterday had some effect. Still, a small-town high school dance decorating party doesn't have that Valentine's Day icky feel. Do you think anyone will mind if I snap a few shots while I'm there? I'm an excellent wedding photographer, but I'm having fun taking pictures of something other than happy couples."

"I'm certain that would be fine."

They spent another two hours at Eternity Springs Community School tying bows, hanging crepe paper flowers, filling latex balloons with helium, and sprinkling candy hearts across the tables. Finally, when the committee head declared the project complete, the volunteers decided their hard work had earned them lunch at Murphy's Pub. Max turned to Ali and asked, "Shall we join them?"

"Aren't you afraid of unwanted attention?"

"There will be enough people around me that I can bury myself in the crowd. Besides, I've learned that my cousin will make a public appearance this afternoon at the festival. So if anyone gives me trouble, I'll tell the truth and direct them to Hummingbird Lake."

Ali slipped her phone from her pocket, checked the time, then shook her head. "You go on. I need to meet Jessica and Sean for the shoot soon, so I'll head back to Aspenglow Place. I saw when we came into the school that it's just down the block."

"Nothing is very far away in Eternity Springs, but I'll walk you back."

"No, you go on. I can walk half a block by myself. This morning was nice, Max. I really enjoyed it."

"Even the crepe paper Valentine hearts here at the gym?"

"Even the crepe paper Valentine hearts."

"Well, good. I'm glad." Max paused a moment, then said, "My mother mentioned you'd asked about using the theater room at Aspenglow Place tonight."

"Yes." She showed him a sheepish grin. "I've promised myself a marathon of horror movies. Jessica thought the B&B had one, but she had mistaken your mother's place for Angel's Rest."

"I have a theater room. Why don't you come to my house? I enjoy a good horror flick. I'll whip up something for dinner or order a pizza if they're not already sold out."

She gave him a sharp look. "Max…"

"Look, how about we officially don't consider it a Valentine's Day date? Would that make you more comfortable?"

"I know it seems silly."

"Hey, I'm the last person to diss anyone for superstitions."

"It's not really a superstition. It's a vow."

"In that case, it's even more understandable. Vows are inviolable."

"Thank you for understanding."

"So, shall I pick you up at seven?"

"To hang out and watch horror movies?"

"And eat dinner."

"On our Not-a-Valentine's-Day Date. How about I bring the popcorn? I assume you have a microwave to nuke it in?"

"I do."

"Okay, then." She nodded. "I'll see you at seven."

Max watched her go and wondered just how much his life was about to change. But no sense worrying about it. What would be, would be. Time would tell. Either she was the woman for him, or she wasn't.

Really, was that any different from the question he had on any first date?

Tonight might not be an official Valentine's Day date, but it darned sure was a date on Valentine's Day. And that was the heart of the matter where the tea leaves were concerned, wasn't it?

Maybe the time had come to give Gabi, at least, a heads up on the Nonnie-Celeste alliance. Because the devil was in the details…no, that's not right. The angel was in the details. Cupid was basically an angel, right?

Romano, you got up wa-a-a-y too early this morning. He pulled out his phone and texted his sister. *Meet me for lunch at Murphy's Pub?*

CHAPTER 9

THIS VALENTINE'S DAY DIDN'T SUCK.

Ali bubbled like the champagne she sipped upon finishing the photoshoot at the thank-you lunch and celebration at Angel's Rest that Sean had arranged. They had a table in a private parlor upstairs in Cavanaugh House with a glorious view of Hummingbird Lake and the kaleidoscope of hot air balloons that remained for the afternoon festivities.

She couldn't wait to get home to see the session's photographs on her monitor. She didn't doubt they'd be spectacular. The shoot today had been nothing short of magical. So much love swirled inside the Beloved Chamber that she easily imagined the stalactite pumped it through invisible arteries and veins encircling the cavern. Even as she enjoyed sharing Jessica and Sean's joy, she couldn't help but feel a little envious.

But her eyes had been opened, too. She'd never had a bring-a-stalactite-to-life sort of love, not even with the man to whom she'd planned to pledge her heart for life.

"So," Jessica said, waggling her brows at Ali. "In your

text message, you said you actually met Luscious Lorenzo? Tell me everything!"

"Well, he flirted with me."

"Eeek!"

Sean smirked and rolled his eyes.

"He danced with me and sang to me."

"Okay, that's a new side of Lorenzo from any I've seen." Sean set down his champagne glass and leaned forward. "Let's hear the details."

She gave them a synopsized and censored version of events. Had she been lunching alone with Jessica, she would have mentioned the naked part of the story, but this wasn't the time or place to describe Max's naked parts. Jessica might swoon, and no sense making Sean feel inferior.

"What?" Jessica asked. She knew Ali well. "Inside joke?"

"I'm laughing at myself." Then, casually, she added, "Max is going to join me for my horror movie marathon tonight. Well, actually, I'm going to join him. He's taking me to his house. He has a theater room. We're going to have pizza and popcorn."

"On Valentine's Day?" Jessica covered her mouth with her hand. "He's talked you into breaking your vow? Oh, my little baby Cupid. I need to meet Max Romano."

"It's not a date," Ali was quick to explain. "We're just hanging out."

Her best friend speared her with a look and shook a dessert fork her way. "Uh-huh. And did you or did you not tell us that he kissed you in the Beloved Chamber?"

"Well…yes."

"And it was the hottest kiss you've ever had?"

"Well…yes…but…."

"And he's picking you up and taking you out for a meal and a movie on Valentine's Day."

"You're making it sound bad. Valentine's Day has nothing to do with it."

"No, Ali. I'm making it sound good! It sounds terrific. Whether you like it or not, today is February fourteenth, and you have a date. Therefore, it sounds to me like you're finally moving past the scum whose name I shall not use but whose favorite golf clubs are now recycled cans holding horrible lite beer. Sean, sweetheart, top off our glasses, would you please? I want to make a toast."

Once the flutes were filled, Ali's best friend lifted her glass and said, "To new beginnings."

"To your new beginning, and my horror flicks." She clinked their glasses.

"Oh, Ali," Jessica whined.

Her friend was still arguing her point later when they entered Aspenglow Place to find the parlor full of females. Maggie Romano introduced her daughter and two daughters-in-law who had joined Maggie and Maggie's grandmother for tea. "Nonnie has been doing readings for us," said Maggie's daughter Gabi. "Would you like to have your tea leaves read?"

Sean begged off, but Jessica jumped right in and was delighted with the process since her reading predicted a happy wedding day. When they turned to Ali, something told her that Maeve Gallagher's readings weren't her cup of tea. She declined by smiling and saying, "Oh, no. No, thank you. I had plenty to drink at lunch."

At first, Ali was worried that she might have offended the women, but they couldn't have been more friendly. In fact, they were almost too friendly. Sean and Jessica escaped upstairs, but the Romano women kept Ali gently hostage with pleasant, friendly conversation. They questioned her using such a subtle touch that she didn't immediately realize she'd undergone an interrogation worthy of a three-letter agency. Then, at some unseen signal, the three younger women rose to leave. They hugged her goodbye and assured her they looked forward to getting to know her better. It was all done with genuine, gushing warmth. This, from a trio of women she'd met twenty minutes ago.

Weird.

And the weirdness wasn't over yet.

Maggie's grandmother—Max's Nonnie—asked if Ali would like her daughter's recipe for Italian cream cake, which all but gave the innkeeper the vapors. Still, she calmed down after her mom said to her, "Eye on the ball, Margaret. He's the last chick. Tea leaves."

Weird, squared.

Ali used her early morning balloon adventure as an excuse to escape upstairs for a nap. The indulgence did her a world of good. If her dreams took her to Renaissance Florence on a romp with a particular naked statue, well, who could blame her?

She slept over two hours, and when she awakened, it was time to get ready for her Valentine's horror hang-out. She showered and shampooed her hair, luxuriating in Aspenglow Place's custom scent of toiletries provided by Heavenscents Soaps. She liked this combination labeled bourbon, mandarin, and vanilla even better than what had been available at the Mine Shack. It was clean and crisp, and at the same time, made your mouth water. She slathered her skin with lotion and wondered if any candy shop anywhere had turned this scent into a cream filling. Wouldn't it make a good chocolate candy?

It's no surprise Maggie would get the best for her place. Ali had learned in the conclave downstairs that Maggie's daughter-in-law Savannah was the genius behind the handmade soaps offered in the local business.

She took a little more time than usual with her hair and makeup, then went to the antique wardrobe to choose her clothes. As she surveyed the limited selections, she reflected on what a lovely day today had been. Never would she have guessed that the only time she'd waste thinking about her ex today would be the moments during lunch when she and Jessica laughed about his golf clubs.

Maybe she was moving on. More likely, Max Romano was just a really great distraction.

She'd pulled on black jeans, a comfy black sweater, and her black leather boots—horror movie night—when a knock sounded on her bedroom door. Expecting it to be Jessica on her way off to her Valentine's Day date, she called, "Come in."

Max's great-grandmother entered her room. "Hello, Maeve."

"I won't keep you, dear. I've been ruminating on our conversation downstairs earlier, and I am compelled to clarify something before you go out with our Max tonight. It's only right. I had hoped to read your leaves first, but well, since Celeste is involved, she brings another level of, well, I would say kismet to the affair. You may have picked up pieces, but you should have the whole of it, don't you think?"

"I don't understand."

"Yes. That's why I'm here. The girls stopped by to welcome you to the family."

Ali scoffed a laugh. "What?"

"Yes. You'll think it's silly, I'm sure. However, don't say we weren't upfront with you. You should know that I read Max's tea leaves this past Thanksgiving. I saw that his Valentine will be his one true love."

Ali waited. "Okay."

"The two of you will marry on Valentine's Day next year."

At that, Ali burst out laughing. She couldn't help it. She didn't want to insult the elderly woman, but seriously. "Mrs. Gallagher, I will admit that your great grandson is a terrific, appealing man. I could even imagine us dating and maybe someday falling in love. However, the one thing I am absolutely positively sure about is that I will never, ever choose Valentine's Day as my wedding day!"

"Yes, dear. We'll see, dear. Now, you go have a good time tonight, Ali, dear." Maeve crooked her fingers for Ali to lean down toward her. She kissed her on the cheek. "You'll make another beautiful Romano bride."

"Oh, for crying out loud," Ali muttered as she shut the door behind the old woman. If her hand trembled a little as she applied her bright red lipstick, well, she darned sure had a reason.

Seven o'clock arrived, and Max did not. Since they apparently did signs around here, maybe she should take his tardiness as one. She was just about to tug her phone from her purse and send him a text when she heard a ding signal an arriving message. It was from Max.

"Running late. Sorry. Dropped off dinner to the widower who lives down the street from me, and he grew chatty. Be there in five."

He took dinner to lonely old men? Okay, she couldn't cancel horror movie night over that.

She wished she'd asked for directions to his house and taken her own car rather than have him pick her up. Maybe that would have headed off some of this "one true love" nonsense.

Well, she should at least meet him outside, so he didn't

come to the door and get her. That would help set the tone for these women here at Aspenglow Place. They were the ones who needed it.

Her plan was thwarted when Jessica came downstairs in search of the lipstick that she'd left in her coat pocket and spied her. "Oh, Ali. You're still here. Good. We wanted to ask you about Monday's ski trip. Sean ran into some friends this afternoon who'd like to join us if that's all right with you?"

"Of course. The more, the merrier."

They discussed the arrangements a couple more minutes, and then her friend hurried back up to her room to complete her preparations. Jessica had seven-thirty dinner reservations with her Valentine at a nearby restaurant. Ali turned toward the front door, and her stomach sank. She was too late. The door opened, and Max sauntered inside, carrying a big bouquet of flowers. And a huge clichéd heart-shaped box of chocolates.

Her stomach sank all the way to her knees. What happened to his hatred of the Day of Hearts?

"Hello, Ali." His appreciative gaze gave her a slow once over. "Black looks good on you."

"Max," she began. "The flowers—"

"Are for my mother," he explained as Maggie Romano walked from the kitchen into the entry hall.

"Oh!" Ali brightened.

Simultaneously, Maggie protested. "Max, no. I'm not your date."

"You're my first love. Happy Valentine's Day, Mom." He handed her the flowers and kissed her on the cheek.

Maggie huffed but smiled. Then she eyed the candy with meaning. Max's eyes gleamed with wicked amusement as he observed, "Mom, did you know that Ali absolutely loves chocolates?"

Maggie beamed. Ali frowned. Max continued, "Of course, so does Nonnie. Where is she?"

"In the kitchen," Maggie answered, her disapproval apparent.

To Ali, he said, "I'll be right back."

While her son disappeared into the kitchen, Maggie stood staring at Ali with her arms full of a red and white rose bouquet, her expression stricken. The sound of her grandmother's cheerful voice floated from the kitchen. "He's always been my grandmother's favorite."

"I understand why." Ali gave her hostess a reassuring smile. "It's sweet of him to bring her chocolates."

"I know, but it's not very romantic for a Valentine's date."

"Maggie, I assure you. Max couldn't have done anything more perfect to begin tonight."

"You mean it?"

"Absolutely." *If you only knew.*

Relief smoothed the tiny lines at the corner of Maggie's eyes. "Good. I'm glad. Maybe he has a box of Valentine's chocolates for you in the car."

"I hope not. Heart-shaped boxes of chocolates are seriously not my thing."

"Really? Why's that?"

"Long story," Ali said as Max came striding out of the kitchen.

"Don't be nosy, Mom. You're a better innkeeper than that. Ali, shall we go? Where's your coat?"

In his truck on the way to his home on Hummingbird Lake, Ali decided to broach the troubling topic before he got too far away from Aspenglow Place. After all, he might turn the truck around and take her back. "Max, you have a problem with your family."

"Wrong tense there, Ali. Definitely should use the plural

form when you're using the nouns 'family' and 'problem' in the same sentence and you are referring to the Romanos."

"Max, I'm serious."

"So am I."

She exhaled a frustrated sigh. "Listen. Please. It's important."

"All right. I'm listening."

"Okay. Well, I don't know if you're aware of this whole tea leaves thing that's going on, but your family is planning your wedding."

He didn't immediately react beyond a slight tightening of his lips. To clarify, Ali said, "*Your* wedding to *me*."

Max sighed heavily. "Yeah, well. I was afraid of that."

"What? You *knew* about it?"

"Here's the deal, Ali. I had an English teacher in seventh grade who taught us to diagram sentences. Do teachers still do that?"

"What does diagramming sentences have to do with this conversation?"

"Punctuation. It's all in the punctuation. You know that joke, 'Let's eat kids?' Or, 'Let's eat *comma* kids?' 'Punctuation saves lives?' Well, in our case, it's not all that different. Nonnie's reading was—and I quote—'Your Valentine will be your one true love.' So, what is missing from the statement? Absolutely any reference to time, that's what."

"You sound like you believe in fortune-telling."

"What I can't deny, because I've seen it with my own two eyes, is that there's something to what my great-grandmother sees in the tea leaves."

"Wow, Max." Ali sat back in her seat. "And here I thought you were so level-headed."

"I know it sounds crazy, but let me tell you about my cousins." He shared the story of Nonnie's readings for

Lorenzo and his siblings. "Those are only three examples. I have a dozen of them."

Ali's thoughts reeled. If she weren't smack dab in the middle of this thing, she'd love digging into the subject and hearing more about these dozen examples. But she *was* in the middle of it. She felt like she needed to protest.

Why? She asked herself.

Well, because. Herself argued back.

Because why?

Now she and herself were back in middle school, apparently. *Wonder if I could get Max as my dreamy tutor so we could diagram sentences together after school.*

"Oh, geez." Ali buried her face in her palms.

"Don't worry," Max said, his tone reassuring. "Seriously. I'm not."

"They're planning our wedding, and we've never been out on a date!"

Max was quiet for a few minutes, then he asked, "Do you have any siblings?"

"No. I'm an only child."

"Do you have any experience at all with big families?"

"None. My parents were both only children. Your family is charming, Max. I don't mean to sound otherwise. But what happened this afternoon is…well…overwhelming."

"I'm sure it was."

Ali had the impression that he intended to say more. Nevertheless, he drove a little farther without speaking. By now, they'd proceeded beyond the town limits and had reached the road that wound alongside Hummingbird Lake. It was a beautiful, clear, crisp winter night. A three-quarter moon and myriad stars shone in an inky sky and gave the snow-covered ground a luminous glow.

Finally, Max spoke. "The Romanos are a big family and

growing bigger all the time. We're Italian on my dad's side and Irish on Mom's. He had six siblings. She has four. Gabi is my only sister, and I have three brothers. We're still working on Tony to move to Eternity Springs."

"I met Savannah and Hope this afternoon."

Max nodded. "Zach's and Lucca's wives. They're fabulous women."

"I liked them. But…."

"They're nosey. It's the Romano way. We tend to stick our noses in each other's business. Still, it's never done maliciously, and we do respect boundaries once they're set. In hindsight, I probably should have set boundaries already where you're concerned."

"See! You are making my point for me. You're all getting way too ahead of yourselves!"

"Yeah, well, that's the Romano way, too. We all played basketball growing up, so the phrase 'Take the ball and run with it' comes naturally to us."

"Max! Aargh! Maybe you'd better just turn this truck around."

"I can do that. Although at this point, it's as quick to make the loop around the lake as to turn around. But give me a minute here, Ali. I'm working my way to a point."

"Maybe you should quicken the pace. Bottom line it, Romano."

"Okay." He pulled the truck into a semicircular drive and braked to a stop in front of a large, traditional log-mountain-cabin-style home. He shifted into park, switched off the engine, then turned to face her. Moonlight combined with landscape lighting illuminated the truck's interior well enough for Ali to see his face.

"I'm a Romano. So, I took the ball and ran."

Oh, no. Trepidation washed over Ali. "What did you do?"

"I tried, Ali. I made a legitimate attempt to keep it casual and order pizza."

She waited. And waited. Eventually, she prodded. "But…?"

He spoke with just enough frustration in his voice to be reassuring. "Like we talked about yesterday, it's the trials of stupid Valentine's Day. Even our pizza place was booked up!"

Oh.

"I promised dinner, so I had no choice but to cook. If I'm going to go to the trouble to cook, it's gonna be good food. You can sue for me that, but that's just the way it is. Now, I can man a grill and a smoker like nobody's business, but when it comes to cooking in the kitchen, my repertoire is limited. I have three dependable dishes, and only one of them is something I can leave to simmer while I go pick up my date."

His date. "Excuse me, but I believe we made it very much a point to say that this isn't a date."

"Well, yeah, we did. But like I told you, Romanos are ballers. So, I'm calling an audible on that."

"You said you play basketball. Aren't audibles called in football? I hope you're not planning to score, Romano. That's another problem I have with Valentine's dates."

"Whoa. Whoa. Whoa. Hold it right there. I have absolutely no expectations beyond horror flicks and popcorn. Do I hope I get a repeat of that kiss? Well, yeah. Of course, I do. That was the hottest kiss I've had in maybe forever. But beyond that…look. If I'd wanted a hook-up, I wouldn't have agreed to hang out. I certainly wouldn't have called the audible."

"So, explain it to me. Why have we gone from not-a-date to a date when neither one of us wanted one?"

"Once I was committed to cooking, well, the whole hanging-out idea fell apart. We can still eat dinner and watch horror movies afterward. That's a perfectly fine way to pass the evening. But it is foolish not to be honest about tonight, Ali. I'd hate to look back and regret it. Perhaps I should have reconsidered the choice of dessert or drawn those boundaries when I shared my suspicions about Celeste's matchmaking efforts and Lorenzo's presence in town. However, this has all happened fast for me, too."

"You've lost me. Maybe I need more than just the bottom line, after all."

"Okay, but let's go inside where it's warm. Get a glass of wine, and we can talk."

"But—" she began to protest.

He placed his index finger against her lip. "If you want to return to Aspenglow Place when I'm finished talking, I'll take you. I'll even fix you a to-go box."

Ali's resistance melted faster than a bucket full of snow dropped into the Mine Shack hot springs pool. She knew she wasn't canceling this, well, whatever this was. But she did want to understand it.

Her heart skipped a little beat when he replaced his finger with a brief brush of his lips. He was out of the truck and around to open her door before she managed to quit thinking about his lips. He led her up the front steps, across a fantastic porch, and inside where she was greeted by delicious aromas and Barney.

After Ali greeted the Newfie, she took a look at Max's home. She vaguely noted the great room with the wall of windows facing the lake, bookcases filled with books, and the chair, ottoman, and lamp positioned perfectly for reading. However, the two-story stone fireplace with dancing flames and the small table set to one side of it captured and held her attention.

Romance with a capital R.

The table was square, sized for two, and artisan-made of gorgeous wood. He'd used cloth placemats and matching napkins threaded through carved wooden rings that matched the table. Beautiful, artistic glass votives that reminded her of the tree toppers in the Beloved Chamber provided the centerpiece.

"May I take your coat?"

She tugged her gaze away from the table to see him standing beside her, his own coat draped over his arm. He wore jeans and a forest green sweater that brought out the color of his eyes. She wondered if he did that consciously. "Nice sweater."

"Thanks. Christmas gift from my mom."

Ali smiled and handed him her coat. "Whatever you are cooking smells fantastic."

"Tuscan chicken. It's keeping happy on the stove. Let's sit by the fire and talk this out, so you can sit down to dinner without anything sour on your taste buds. Would you like a glass of wine?"

"I would, thank you."

He gestured for her to take a seat on the sofa in front of the enormous stone fireplace. She sat watching the fire until he joined her carrying a tray holding a bottle of wine, two glasses, and a charcuterie board. He set the tray on a coffee table beside an antique rose bowl with fresh flowers—one yellow rose surrounded by half a dozen white ones.

Max sat beside her on the sofa, poured the wine, and handed her a glass. "Happy Valentine's Day, Ali Lovejoy."

To her surprise and dismay, her throat grew tight. She blinked back tears. "You have made it one, Max. Thank you.

Now, could you go back to the bottom line and make this all make sense to me?"

"I'll try." He snagged a piece of cheddar from the board. "Where was I?"

"Changing the play."

"Right. Okay." He took a bite of his cheese and gathered his thoughts. "Evidence leads me to put stock into my great-grandmother's readings. Evidence also leads me to suspect that Celeste Blessing dabbled in a little matchmaking magic yesterday, and she's darn sure good at it."

"She set us up at Mistletoe Mine?"

"I think she did, yes."

Ali furrowed her brow. "I don't understand. I don't know Celeste Blessing. She doesn't know me. I mean, Jessica may have told her about me. But the first time we actually met was yesterday when I climbed into her golf cart."

"Which supports my point."

"What point?"

"That none of it matters. Not the tea leaves reading, not my family's wedding planning, and not Celeste's matchmaking. They shouldn't bother you. They don't bother me."

"Because I live in Texas?"

"No, that's something that can be overcome. But, look, Ali, back to this bottom line. Something brought us together yesterday—call it fate, destiny, or Cupid's magical arrows—I don't know. But that's as far as it goes. That's where it stops. We're driving the bus now. You and I are in control from here on out."

"How is that?"

"Because no fate or destiny or magic took hold of my tongue and made me ask you out. That was all me. My idea. I asked you out. On a date. A date that just happens to be on

Valentine's Day. I bought flowers for you because I like to give flowers to my dates."

Ali went still. "You bought me flowers?"

He gestured toward the rose bowl. "These are for you. I wasn't going to take them to Aspenglow Place and give them to you in front of my mother."

He bought her flowers. She wasn't supposed to like the fact that he bought her flowers because this was stupid, horrible, detestable Valentine's Day. However, she had to blink away the wetness in her eyes and clear her throat again before she spoke. "They're beautiful."

"It's the yellow rose of Texas surrounded by the Colorado snow." As Ali reached out to trace the cut glass with her index finger, Max added, "My mom gave me the vase a few years ago. It was Nonnie's."

Appalled, she jerked her hand back. "Max, no. You can't."

"I darn sure can." He reached for her hand and held it. "I thought it had a nice symmetry." He brought her hand to his mouth and kissed it.

"But—"

"Stop it. Look, even if our first date ends up being our only date, I hope you'll have a nice memory of it. There's no reason you should have Nightmare on Valentine's Day II, right? I mean, even if the chicken turns out lousy…." He lowered his voice to a sensual rumble. "I have dessert."

CHAPTER 10

"DESSERT?" SHE BREATHED.

The kiss was but a whisper, the softest brush of his lips against hers. Now that he'd finally surrendered to the urge that had hummed through him since before the sun came up this morning, he wanted to take his time and draw the pleasure out. Her lips were delightfully soft and blissfully moist.

Sweet. Delicious. *Oh, Ali Lovejoy, you are delectable,* he thought.

It would be so easy to deepen the kiss, to slide his tongue into that soft, wet mouth and lose himself in the taste of her.

And he'd better slow down, or he'd totally spoil his supper.

And yet, he needed one more minute. So, he dabbled, learning, playing, fascinated by the sense of familiarity. Okay, this *was* their second kiss. Although, most details of that first time were lost to a haze of hormonal lust.

Not that it would take more than about half a second to get to that level of lust again. *Better cool your jets, Romano.*

Kissing Ali Lovejoy felt like coming home. Like this was meant to be. Like she was his destiny.

Whoa. Was it hubris to think that he and Ali were driving the bus now? Or were they really just along for the ride?

Max didn't know whether to laugh or groan, but he did think it probably best to keep that question to himself for the time being. So, he reluctantly ended the kiss and prepared to make a different query.

"So, Ali." The soft glow of firelight cast a golden light across her flushed cheeks and kiss-moistened lips. She opened arousal-drugged eyes and looked at him. He could drown in those eyes. *Oh, how I want her.* "Will you stay?"

"For dinner and a movie?"

Forever. "For our first date."

"That just happens to be on Valentine's Day."

My Valentine will be my one true love. "That just happens to be on Valentine's Day."

"What movie are we going to watch?"

He couldn't not touch her, so he stroked his thumb across her cheek. "You said horror. Titanic? Dirty Dancing? The Notebook? 27 Dresses? How to Lose a Guy in 10 Days?"

She punched him in the stomach. "Funny guy."

He grinned. This was good. It broke the tension, so he just might get his Tuscan chicken served after all. "Oh, wait. Horror doesn't mean chick flick in your lexicon? So then, since it's a holiday, how about Halloween?"

"I don't know." Ali lifted her shoulders in a shrug, then chose a walnut from the charcuterie board and popped it into her mouth. "I'm not feeling it. Since we did the classic movie thing yesterday…."

"Now you're talking," Max replied with enthusiasm. "Alfred Hitchcock? The Birds? Tippi Hedren was hot."

"That's a good one. What are our other choices?"

They discussed Hitchcock movies at length during dinner, discovering they both loved classic films and had extensive knowledge upon which to draw. His chicken was a hit, as usual, and when they'd finished their meal, he carried their plates to the kitchen and asked Ali to bring the wine. While Max quickly and efficiently scraped the dishes and loaded his dishwasher, the conversation moved to foodie movies. Coming up with titles they both had seen in this category proved to be more challenging.

Ali frowned over her wine, then snapped her fingers. "I've got one. Surely you've seen *Chocolat?*

"Skipped it to watch *Butter.*"

She laughed. "Was there really a movie named *Butter?*"

"Oh, yeah. It was pretty good. But then, it's butter. How do you screw up butter? Which is a nice segue to dessert. Shall we have it now up here, or do we take it with us down to the theater room and have it later?"

"I'm stuffed. Let's have it later."

"Sounds like a plan." He handed her a bakery box and spoke in a solemn tone. "Whatever you do, don't drop this."

"Can I peek?"

"Not until you're safely downstairs. If you drop it, Barney will be on it quick as a minute, and he'll eat all of it. I might have to keep the flowers in that case because our date will be ruined."

She giggled at that. Actually giggled. "I guess I'll wait and let it be a surprise."

"It won't be a surprise, Ali. It'll be a religious experience."

"Okay, I have to know. Just what is this miracle dessert?"

Reverently, Max said, "Italian cream cake."

"Huh. Did your mother make it?"

"Yes. It's for a family party tomorrow at my sister's house, but I sweet-talked her out of two pieces for tonight. How did you know?"

"Your mom gave me the recipe this afternoon."

Max fumbled the bakery box. Lying on his favorite bed in the theater room corner, Barney lifted his head and thumped his tail. Ali made the save and caught the box before it spilled.

"Everything okay?" she asked.

"Yeah. That one caught me off guard, is all." Considering that his mother hadn't yet given the recipe to Gabi or any of her daughters-in-law, yeah. He was shocked out of his socks.

"This is an awesome room," Ali said as she set the cake box on the counter of the mini-kitchen.

"Thanks. It has all the necessities—a microwave, kegerator, and fridge with enough counter space for a large pizza and cabinet space to hide the paper plates and trash can." He rattled off the sound and video specs, which didn't seem to interest her, and finished with, "The john is through that door."

She crossed the room to give Barney a little attention while Max finished setting up for the movie part of their dinner-and-a-movie date. He'd made some preparations in the theater room before picking up Ali for their date. Ordinarily, individual reclining seats furnished the room and were used when Max and his brothers got together to watch sports. Today he'd rearranged the seating, moving the indies to the back row and placing the two-person loveseat front and center before the enormous screen. In addition, Max had extended the snack trays built into each arm.

Now he opened a sparkling, spritzy Moscato di Asti that paired wonderfully with the cake. He set a piece of cake and glass of wine on each snack tray, then sat in the loveseat and gestured for Ali to join him. Not content with space in between them, he snuggled her up against him. "All right. Back to the movie. What have you decided, Shutterbug?

Which direction are we going? Halloween or Hitchcock? What's it gonna be?"

She cleared her throat. "Actually, I was thinking…what about…maybe…*Roman Holiday?*"

Max leaned away from her and gave her a long look. "Well, Ali Lovejoy. I do believe you've made a breakthrough."

"Is that okay?"

"Hmm, I don't know. If I recall the plot, the female lead goes off to a beautiful, exciting new place and meets her true love? How hokey is that? That said, I'm happy to watch Audrey Hepburn any day of the week."

Grinning, she settled back into his arms. Max picked up the remote, did a bit of searching, found the movie, and started to stream.

Gregory Peck had just taken Audrey back to his apartment when Ali reached over, picked up her fork, and took a bite of nirvana. She sat up straight. "Oh, my."

Max paused the movie. "Good, isn't it? You know, men have literally gone to war over Mom's Italian cream cake."

She took a second bite. "That's sinful."

"We prefer heavenly in the Romano household. It's Celeste's influence." Max picked up his own piece, and because he simply didn't have any discipline where this particular dessert was concerned, he wolfed it down.

Ali, on the other hand, tortured him by eating slowly, savoring every bite. She closed her eyes, licked her lips. Licked. Her. Fork. And she still had half of her piece to eat.

Enough of that. Max tugged her fork out of her hand and tossed it aside. "Max!"

He broke off a piece of cake and held it to her lips. "Now do me."

What followed was the most intense culinary sensual—or

sensual culinary—three minutes of his life. Their gazes locked, Ali touched only Max's finger and thumb with her teeth, lips, and tongue. By the time she'd sucked the last little bit of frosting from his skin, he'd broken out into a sweat, and he was hard as Rocky Mountain granite.

"That's better than a box of chocolates. I'm going to have to make that cake."

"Oh, yeah."

She reached for her wine and settled back against him. "Restart the movie, Max."

He shifted in his seat, trying to get comfortable, feeling around for the remote. In the meantime, Ali scooped it off the floor where he'd dropped it. After pressing play, she retained possession of the device. He was so addled that he didn't register a protest. Neither did he realize that she was strung as tightly as he until, just when Audrey was buying a pair of shoes in Rome, Ali thumbed the pause button and leaped to her feet. She whirled around to face him.

Her eyes looked a little wild. Her voice sounded a little shrill. "Before this goes on one minute longer, Max Romano, you need to know the truth."

"Okay. What truth?"

"Why I hate Valentine's Day!

CHAPTER 11

"I've been a porn star all my life."

Max blinked. "Come again?"

"Well, not literally." Ali waved her hand.

"Thank God for that."

Her heart pounding, she began to pace. It was a secret she'd sworn never to share again. Every time. Every. Single. Time. She'd ended up being hurt. So why was she doing this? Now? Why was she going to ruin what up until now had been the best Valentine's Day of her entire life?

Because this had been the best Valentine's Day of her life.

And girls like her didn't get to have nice things. Nice boyfriends. Nice fiancés. Nice first dates on Valentine's Day.

And right now, she had her hopes up. Great big huge hopes, hanging up high like mistletoe in the mine. Right next to a heart named Beloved. Rocky Mountain high hopes.

Well, knock 'em down. Take a bat to 'em like a piñata.

When he laughed at her, belittled her, or cavalierly told her to change it without bothering to ask why she hadn't done so already, he'd be one more in a long line of callous jerks. Then, Max's reaction would tell her everything she needed to know about how much fantasizing to devote to this fantasy night.

Tell him. Do it. Do it now. Get it over with before this goes on another glorious minute.

She halted, folded her arms, and confessed. "It's my name! My legal name! I'm Valentine Lovejoy!"

She waited for the guffaw. It didn't come. Neither did the smirk or the wink or the elbow in the side. Or the lewd and crude gestures. The rude jokes. The Google searches. The porn sites…just no.

What he did do shocked her. He nodded. "Ah. Yes, I get it. Totally. I totally understand."

Her chin came up. Okay, that wasn't as bad, but it was *almost* as bad. "No, you don't."

"I sure do." Max rose from his seat, folded his arms, and squared off in front of her. "*My* full first name is Maximus."

"Maximus?" Ali froze.

"Uh-huh. Maximus. And, yes, Valentine, I've heard condom jokes all my life. So, I'd say that gives me a fair understanding as to what being the butt of porn star jokes is like."

Okay, she couldn't argue with that. Ali's hands dropped to her sides. Her heart continued to race, but the reason why had changed. *He's a nice guy. And this has been a fabulous first date. A fabulous Valentine's Date.*

Max pulled her into his arms. "I'm named after my grandfather. You?"

"My mother's twin sister. She died when they were twelve."

"That's a beautiful testimonial." He nuzzled her hair. "And you know, it's actually a beautiful name, too. It's a crying shame to let dirty-minded people sully it."

"I know. That's come in waves throughout my life. Kids

can be cruel. I thought I'd outgrown it, but then last year...." She shrugged.

"Mr. Valentine himself. Enough said." He nipped her ear in silent rebuke. "You know, this little bit of information only goes further to convince me that Nonnie and Celeste may be onto something. Maybe we really are a perfect match."

"Max, we've known each other two days!"

"Well, time will tell, won't it? I suggest we take it one day at a time. One date at a time."

"But your family is planning our wedding!"

"Oh, don't worry about them. Believe me, tomorrow at a family dinner, Lorenzo is putting on a big production to surprise my mother with the announcement of her heart's desire. My sister is having a baby, and it's a girl, and there's all this Gallagher family history to the production. Nonnie and Celeste are involved. Anyway, any ideas about wedding planning will evaporate the moment the "b" word is voiced."

"Oh, I take it your sister is thrilled?"

"Delirious." Max began nibbling his way down her neck. "You're delicious."

A shiver of desire raced up Ali's spine. "Are we going to finish the movie?"

"I know how it ends." He captured her mouth in a long, steamy kiss. "And they all live happily ever after. Except with this one, you need to use your imagination a bit."

"That's why I like romances. They always have a happy ending."

"Want to hear a secret?"

"Sure. I'd like that. I told you one of mine. A big one."

"I told you one of mine, too. A maximum one."

Ali snorted.

Max kissed her again, then said, "I like romances, too. It's fun to travel along with characters and watch them fall in love throughout a story, whether a book, a television series, or a movie. Except for *Riviera.* I don't like watching Lorenzo's character fall in love."

Ali laughed. "I like watching Gregory Peck."

"And Audrey. Shall we watch the rest of *Roman Holiday?* You know, we could subtitle our Valentine's Day date *Eternity Springs Holiday.*"

"I like that. No sense in fast-forwarding."

"Good. And I agree on the fast-forwarding. We might miss some of the good parts."

"We wouldn't want to do that."

"No, we absolutely wouldn't want to do that. We have plenty of time." He sat and pulled her onto his lap. While "Joe" and "Ann" kissed on an Italian riverbank, Max and Ali followed suit on a loveseat in a theater room in Colorado.

By the time the end credits ran on both the movie and their Valentine's Day date, they'd completely lost track of time. He took her back to Aspenglow Place a little before midnight. "Let me help you with your flowers," he said as he helped her from his truck. Then, as he walked her to the front door, he added, "Do you see that every window curtain in the place is fluttering?"

"They're spying on us?"

"From their bedrooms. They'll probably congregate in the parlor when we walk onto the porch. They'll want to watch for the goodnight kiss."

Ali stifled a smile. "Poor Jessica will feel left out."

"Nah. Mom's an excellent hostess. She'll invite her to join them."

"Oh. Well, that's nice." Then, after a moment's pause, she added, "This makes me feel sixteen again."

"Yep. Me, too. It's really weird when you take a girl home from a date, and the home you're taking her to is your mother's house. This is a first for me. Can't say I'm down with it, dawg. I am definitely not dating my sister!"

She laughed. "You didn't have to walk me to the door."

"And hear about it the rest of our lives? I don't think so." Max placed his hand at the small of Ali's back and escorted her up the front steps of Aspenglow Place.

At the front door, they stopped, and she turned to face him. "I can't believe I'm actually saying this, but I hate to see today end. This has been a magical Valentine's Day, Max. Thank you for the wonderful day."

"Thank you, Ali." He set her flowers on a plant stand near the front door, then took her into his arms. "I had a great time. Best first date ever."

She wrapped her hands around his neck and lifted her face. He was so tall that she had to go up on tip-toes. "So, what's it gonna be? Do we make this short and sweet for privacy's sake, or do you channel your inner Lorenzo to give them a show?"

"Shutterbug. Please. If I want to plant an Oscar-winning kiss on you, no acting will be involved. It'll be one hundred percent real."

"I don't think the Oscars have a category for kissing."

"That's the excuse my cousin gives my aunt for being caught practicing so much."

"She falls for that?"

"No, but it helps her save face at her bridge club. So, now, the kiss? Peck or a plant?"

"Wait. Wait. Wait. I want a plant, please, but I'd like a bit of a script since we have an audience. I assume you're going for iconic, but are we talking a *The Notebook* kiss? *Breakfast at Tiffany's? Casablanca?*"

"No script, Shutterbug. Remember?"

"I just think I'd be more comfortable with a script."

"We could choose one, but face it, once we get to work on the plant, we're both going to forget our lines."

"You have a point."

From the far corner of the porch, a window slid open. Max's great-grandmother said, "Maximus, would you hurry up and kiss the girl? My bunion is killing me."

"Yes, Nonnie," he replied, laughter in his tone and a twinkle in his voice.

He captured Ali's mouth and swept her away to South Carolina, New York City, and Morocco. She flew the entire distance, her feet never touching the ground.

When he finally released her and stepped back, Ali slowly returned to earth. "Wow." She filled her lungs with air and then exhaled sharply. "You'd snatch the Oscar right out from beneath your cousin's nose."

Max flashed a grin and tipped an imaginary hat. "So, when can I see you again, Ali?"

The question took a sharp pin to her happy bubble. "I'd love to see you again, Max, but how could it possibly work? I live in Texas, and you live in Colorado. We both own businesses that require weekend work."

"Wednesday is a great day for a date. Bracket it with a Tuesday and a Thursday, and you've got yourself a nice bit of together time. So, since we're doing snow and cold for our first date, how does a beach sound for date number two? Right before Spring Break? The Florida Keys? Hawaii?"

"Hawaii!" She blinked. "Isn't that rather extravagant for a second date?"

"You deserve extravagance."

The memory of a Valentine's stash of perfume, jewelry, lingerie, and a teddy bear flashed through her mind. "I don't need or want extravagance, Max. That's not who I am."

"Oh, I'd figured that out by the time you picked up a pair

of scissors and started cutting construction paper hearts in the Eternity Springs Community School gymnasium. Maybe I misspoke. *We* need extravagance. Think about it. Sun, sand, surf, umbrella drinks." He brushed her lips with his. From inside the house came the sound of a crash and feminine giggles. "No family within hundreds of miles…."

Valentine Lovejoy went up on her tiptoes and gave Maximus Romano a quick, hard kiss. "It's a date."

EPILOGUE

Angel's Rest Healing Center and Spa
Eternity Springs, Colorado

On the morning of February fifteenth, Celeste Blessing brewed a pot of High Mountain oolong tea, a delicious gift from her dear friend, Maeve Gallagher. She placed her teapot, cup, and saucer on a tray and carried them to her office, setting the tray on her desk. Ordinarily, Celeste didn't work on Sunday mornings. But then, the task she anticipated awaiting her wouldn't precisely be classified as work now, would it? She more rightly considered it to be the reward for a job well done.

She sat in her chair, poured a cup of tea, and nudged her computer mouse. Her monitor lit up. She logged into the resort's system and navigated to the reservations section, special requests form page.

One new message, sent at one forty-two a.m. this morning.

Room Request: The Mine Shack.

Date: February 14th, next year.

Guest: Mr. and Mrs. Max Romano.

Celeste smiled, sipped her tea, and sent a confirmation number: TEAMVALENTINE.

She was about to shut off her computer when a second special request caught her notice. “Well, well, well. Max, you sneaky dog.”

Celeste sat back in her chair, lost in thought, while she finished her cup of tea. Then she picked up her phone.

Celeste Blessing had some decorating to do.

THE SUMMER MELT

AN EXCERPT

~

Chapter One

Something cold and wet landed on Dana Delaney's hands as she unlocked the back door of Scoops, her ice cream parlor in Eternity Springs, Colorado. Glancing above her, she grimaced. Snowflakes? Seriously? It was the seventeenth of May!

"Double Chocolate Toffee Crunch," she muttered, cursing in her own particular way. Nothing like springtime in the Rockies.

It might just send her to the poorhouse.

She stepped inside her shop, flipped on the lights, and stowed her purse and lunch tote in her office. Glancing at the wall clock, she read eleven fifty-one. She had nine minutes to complete the short list of daily tasks required before opening the store.

Not that she needed to worry about a rush of customers at noon. Oh, she would see her handful of daily customers, but unfortunately, this type of weather didn't bring in tourists and townspeople the way sunshine and warm weather did.

She needed sunshine and warm weather and tourists this summer. Lots of tourists. Lots and lots and lots of tourists.

Dana sighed heavily and went about her prep. She opened the front door at three minutes to noon and carried her broom outside to sweep off the sidewalk. An occasional snowflake continued to swirl in the gusty breeze. As she bent to sweep debris into her dustpan, a familiar voice called her name. Dana straightened and smiled to see her friend, Celeste Blessing, crossing Spruce Street from the Mocha Moose, holding a lidded paper cup in each hand.

Celeste was the owner of Angel's Rest Healing Center and Spa. Now a thriving resort, Angel's Rest had breathed new life into Eternity Springs when the small mountain town was in danger of dying. Celeste was exceedingly kind, beyond generous, and wise in ways that benefited all those who requested her counsel and advice. She had become the town's happiness ambassador. For Dana, Celeste filled the hole created by the passing of Dana's beloved mother and maternal grandmother.

Today, just like most days, Celeste sparkled. She wore a matching gold rain jacket and hat over skinny jeans. Her light blue eyes gleamed from beneath the wide-brimmed rain hat that sat jauntily atop her short, silver-gray hair. Her smile made the overcast day seem brighter. "Happy Tuesday, Dana," she said. "Do you have a few minutes for a cup of tea and a chat? I have a business proposition for you."

"I absolutely have time." Only a fool would be too busy to listen to a business proposition from Celeste Blessing. The woman had uncanny instincts.

Chimes jingled as Dana opened the door and gestured for her friend to proceed her into the shop. Celeste took a seat at one of the half dozen red-and-white-striped parlor sets that served as seating inside Scoops. After dumping the contents of her dustpan and stowing her broom, Dana joined her.

"I guess it's more a favor than a proposition," Celeste began, scooting one of the paper cups across the table toward Dana. "It's about one of my summer employees. Have you met Rusk Buchanan?"

The name sounded vaguely familiar to Dana, but she couldn't place him. "I don't believe so."

"He's one of my study abroad students."

Then it clicked. The Colorado Rockies teemed with international students during the summer. "Oh, is he the guy that the teens in town are calling the 'Hot Scot'? I overheard the high school cheerleading team talking about him when they stopped in for ice cream last week. He's in one of the college programs but he's got the high school girls in a tizzy."

"That's him." Celeste sipped her tea, nodded, and sighed. "He's a sweetheart and an excellent worker. I hired him to lifeguard at the resort swimming pool, but it's not working out. Yesterday alone, we had three incidents of false cougar drownings."

Dana frowned. "False cougar drownings?"

"It's not just the high school girls who are in a tizzy. Females at least a decade older than Rusk who go into the pool—where the water is still quite chilly, mind you—and pretend to struggle to be rescued by a wet 'Hot Scot.'"

"Oh." Dana couldn't help but chuckle. "Oh, dear."

"Yes, oh dear. And that's only the older women. Once school lets out and the summer tourist season begins in earnest, my fear is that the swimming pool will be overrun. I don't want to have to close it to locals or institute a lottery system for daily entrance."

"That would be a shame." The Angel's Rest swimming pool was the only public pool in town, and it's where the majority of the children in Eternity Springs learned to swim.

"It's quite the conundrum. I would shift Rusk into a different job at the resort, except that would leave me short one lifeguard, and it's late in the season to be finding someone qualified."

"That's true," Dana agreed. Eternity Springs was a

geographically isolated small town. Finding help was always a problem. Finding specialized help could be a nightmare.

"I have thought of one possible solution, but it involves you. So that's where the favor comes in."

Dana knew what Celeste was about to say, and her stomach sank. "You want to poach my assistant manager."

When Dana opened Scoops four years ago, Alissa Cooper had been sixteen and her first hire. She was intelligent, dependable, and trustworthy. She'd been a godsend for Dana.

She also was a certified lifeguard.

Celeste held up her hand, palm out. "Not poach. Hear me out, Dana. I know how much you count on Alissa. What I'm proposing is a trade. Rusk for Alissa. Of course, they'd both need to agree to the change, but based on comments Rusk has made, I feel confident he'd be on board. I didn't want to approach Alissa before I spoke to you. However, I suspect she'd like the job. You know how much she loves our pool. Last summer, she swam laps almost every morning before work."

It was true. Alissa would love to spend her summer outdoors. However, Dana identified one insurmountable problem. Grimacing, she said, "Oh, Celeste. I can't match Angel's Rest's pay scale."

Especially not this year, she thought, what with the bank loan she'd taken out last fall she had coming due at summer's end.

Dana wasn't getting wealthy with her ice cream parlor, but she made a decent living from it. And, she loved the lifestyle Eternity Springs offered. Ordinarily, she could withstand a year of bad weather. However, last fall she'd chosen to make a substantial donation to help with medical expenses for her oldest and dearest friend's seven-year-old son. Dana didn't regret incurring the debt for a minute, even if it did mean she had to sweat snowfall in May. Seven-year-old Logan Ellison had received his new kidney and was doing great.

"No worries, there. Angel's Rest will cover the difference. However, I don't think you've grasped the big picture, Dana. Think about it. Cougars eat ice cream, too."

"Oh. *Cougars.*" Dana sat back in her chair. The beginnings of a smile flickered on her mouth as she gazed through the shop's large picture frame window to the dreary, overcast afternoon. "Even when it's chilly, you think?"

Celeste's blue eyes twinkled over the cup she brought to her mouth for a sip of tea. "I have a hunch that Scoops will have a banner season with Rusk serving up dips of Royal Gorgeous Gumdrop."

"Okay then. I know better than to bet against one of your hunches. I'll talk to Alissa when she comes in. I'd also like to visit with your study abroad student."

"I anticipated that. I invited Rusk to stop in for an ice cream cone at twelve twenty."

Dana glanced at the clock on the wall and read twelve seventeen just as a tall, broad figure strode past the front window. "Celeste, you are a wonder."

The door's bells chimed, and a young man stepped inside. He nodded toward Celeste, then met Dana's gaze and smiled. *Whoa. Hot Scot, indeed.*

Rusk Buchanan was the very cliché of tall, dark and handsome, and his smile had enough wicked in it to tempt any female with a pulse. So, when his heavy-lidded green eyes focused on Dana, she instinctively wanted to preen—until he called her ma'am during the introductions.

"It put me in my place," Dana explained to her friend Amy Elkins when they met for a happy-hour drink after work.

"And reminded me that he's barely old enough to buy me a drink! He's an awfully cute fella though. If a Hollywood scout ever discovered him, he could easily be America's next heartthrob."

Rusk started work at Scoops the following day. By week's end and despite the lingering cold spell, Dana's daily sales had tripled. The young man quickly proved to be a collegiate champion flirt while working behind the safety barrier provided by the display case.

Warmer weather finally arrived and settled in with Memorial Day Weekend. Dana extended operating hours from nine to nine. Rusk worked the day shift, and Dana regularly arrived in the morning to find a line outside the door.

As the days ticked by, Dana worked long hours, stepping up production to keep up with demand, happy as a clam to be doing it. She had yet to begin dating again following the breakup of a longtime relationship last year, so putting in extra time at Scoops suited her perfectly. At the close of business each day, she made a silent toast to Celeste when she counted her receipts. If sales continued at this pace, she'd have her loan paid off by the Fourth of July.

Everything changed the second week of June when her phone rang at eight a.m. and Rusk Buchanan whispered, "Dana, I am unwell. I will not make my shift today."

"Oh, no! What's the matter?"

"I think the fairies came calling while I slept. They drove over me with a truck, banged my head with a hammer, and scraped my throat raw with a zester."

"Oh, Rusk. I'm so sorry. Do you have a fever?"

"No, but I do have a strange rash on my belly. I'm to see the doctor in a wee bit. I am sorry to leave you in the lurch."

"Don't worry about that." Though Dana couldn't help but have a flutter of concern. She'd had a horrible sore throat, fatigue, and a rash when she had mononucleosis in college. The illness put her down for the count for three whole weeks. "Follow the doctor's orders and concentrate on taking care of yourself. Get well soon, Rusk."

"I'll do my best. I will miss my daily dairy fix."

Dana decided she wasn't about to let her Highland Hottie do without. Arriving at Scoops early, she packed a half dozen pints of his favorite flavor and headed for his address, a garage apartment that Celeste provided at one of her rental properties. Dana climbed the wooden staircase to the apartment above the garage and knocked on the door. "Rusk? Special delivery. Pike's Peach is guaranteed to tickle your tastebuds and soothe your sore—"

The door swung open, and an invisible mule kicked the air right out of Dana's lungs. Because a stranger wearing nothing but gym shorts, sneakers, and sweat stood gazing at her with a curious look.

"Throat," Dana croaked. Actually, abs. A sculpted six-pack of them, covered by a light dusting of hair that arrowed downward to disappear into his shorts. And, *whoa,* she jerked her gaze upward, but it got stuck on shoulders. She'd always had a thing for broad shoulders on a man, and his spanned an area as wide as the front range of the Rockies.

He wasn't Rusk. He was a bigger, brawnier version of Rusk. An older version of Rusk.

Dana's new employee spoke of his family often. This must be his older brother, the former professional baseball player who had moved to Florida to live with their grandparents during high school. He now made his living as a highly successful sports agent. His name was Cal, she believed. Short for Calum.

Oh, wow. This Buchanan man was definitely old enough to buy her a drink.

Dana got a taste of the Hot Scot hormone rush that had tripled Scoops' sales so far this summer. Her heartbeat fluttered like a hummingbird's wings.

And that was before the slow, sexy smile softened his chiseled jawline, and his dark green eyes gave her an appreciative once over. Her mouth went dry.

Then he spoke. "May I help you?"

Hearing a faint echo of Rusk's Scottish burr emerge from Cal Buchanan's mouth spiked the temperature of the heat flushing through her. She feared her Pike's Peach might just melt all over the landing.

Wordlessly, she held up the basket.

His gaze focused on the ice cream pints in the basket she carried. Those gorgeous green eyes lit with pleasure, and Even Hotter Scot said, "Ah. You must be Dana Delicious."

Read on for an excerpt of the first novella in the
Celebrate Eternity Springs series.
THE CHRISTMAS PAWDCAST

THE CHRISTMAS PAWDCAST

AN EXCERPT

Chapter One

Dallas, Texas

"Carol of the Bells" drifted from the sound system and blended with the laughter of the holiday party guests who were taking their leave. Mary Landry worked to keep the smile on her face as she hugged and cheek-kissed and waved goodbyes to the stragglers. She had enjoyed the party, and she was thrilled that so many invited guests had attended. But seriously, would these people never go home? She still had so much to do! How could it possibly already be December twentieth?

"Tonight was so much fun," bubbled a wedding planner from Plano, her blue eyes sparkling with champagne. "Landry and Lawrence Catering throws the best party of the season, year in and year out. Thanks so much for inviting us!"

"I'm so glad you could join us." Mary graciously accepted

the woman's enthusiastic hug and glanced up at her date. "Shall I call an Uber for y'all?"

"We're good," he said. "I'm the designated driver tonight, but I can't say I missed the booze. Your non-alcoholic eggnog was killer."

"Mary is the best chef in Dallas," the wedding planner declared. "Restaurants are always trying to lure her into their kitchens."

"Mary! Great party!" A venue manager sailed toward them, which helped ease the first couple out the door. "I don't know what tweak you made to your mac-and-cheese recipe, but it made the exquisite simply divine."

She hadn't changed a thing. "Thank you, Liz."

"You gonna share your recipe?"

"Nope. Trade secrets."

"Dang it. Although my waistline and arteries both thank you for that. Merry Christmas, Mary."

"Merry Christmas."

Finally, almost an hour after the party had been scheduled to end, Mary's business partner Eliza Lawrence shut the door behind the last guest. She gave her long brown hair a toss and flourished her arms like a game show hostess. "We are so freaking awesome!"

Mary laughed. "Yes, we are."

"I do believe tonight even topped last year's party, which I didn't think would be possible."

"Everything went like clockwork—except getting guests to depart."

Eliza waved her hand dismissively. "That's the sign of a successful event. You know that."

Mary nodded. It was why their Christmas event was the one party of the year where Eliza, the logistics director of their business, loosened her timeline.

"Everyone raved about the food as usual," Eliza continued, "but the shrimp balls were a particular hit. You outdid yourself with those, Mary. The vendors who were here tonight are going to talk them up to their clients. We'll be up to our elbows in shrimp all next year."

"I figured they'd be a hit. Nothing has topped my maple mac-and-cheese, though. I think that was all gone by nine o'clock."

"The Landry and Lawrence classic." Eliza sighed happily. "You ready for a glass of champagne? I built time for champagne into our schedule. The cleanup crew doesn't arrive for forty minutes."

"I'm more than ready." Mary's thoughts returned to her to-do list, and she winced. "Mind drinking it in my office? I need to finish my dad's gift before I head home tonight."

Eliza chastised her with a look.

"I know. I know."

Her partner reached out and gave Mary a quick hug. "I'll grab a bottle and glasses and meet you in your office on one condition."

Mary's mouth twisted in a crooked smile. "What's that?"

"Change your clothes before you break out the hot glue gun. I don't want to be taking you to the ER with third-degree boob burns five days before Christmas."

Mary snorted.

"I think I heard almost as many comments on how great you looked tonight as I heard about how fantastic the shrimp balls tasted. It's a spectacular dress, Mar. I'm glad you decided to show off your curves for a change. Emerald is your color. It brings out your eyes. I swear, when Travis arrived and got a look at you, I thought he was going to swallow his tongue."

"Because I'm wearing last year's Christmas gift." Mary

fingered the teardrop garnet pendant that nestled against her breasts. "He accidentally left it off the list of things he asked me to return when he dumped me."

Eliza wrinkled her nose. "If I said it once, I said it a thousand times. The man is a dewsh. I know we couldn't cut him from the guest list because he does own three wedding venues in the Metroplex, but I honestly didn't think he'd have the nerve to show up with her in tow."

"Oh, I knew they'd be here." That's why she'd made such an effort with her outfit tonight.

"Well, you definitely won tonight's skirmish. Raylene sailed in here dressed in her slinky silver sequins, holding her nose in the air and flashing her rock, but you put her in her place without so much as a 'Bless your heart,' just by being gracious."

"She's a beautiful woman."

"And you're a natural red-headed pagan goddess—who will find somebody worthy of you. Trust me, you dodged a bullet by getting rid of that creep."

Emotion closed Mary's throat, and tears stung her eyes. How was it that Eliza always knew just the right thing to say? While she'd put Travis Trent behind her, and she hadn't cried over him in over five months, seeing him tonight hadn't been easy. No woman enjoyed seeing her ex parade her replacement around in front of her. Especially not in her own place of business. Clearing her throat, Mary tried to lighten the subject by saying, "I was aiming for sexy Santa's helper."

"Honey, I wouldn't be surprised to find a dozen men in red suits and white beards lined up outside our door when we leave here tonight."

Mary laughed. What would she do without her best friend? "Oh, Eliza. I do love you."

"I love you, too. Now go cover up that fabulous rack so

you can finish your dad's gift. I'm going to change, too, and then I'll grab the bubbly and meet you in your office."

Ten minutes later, armed with a hot glue gun and wearing jeans, a sweatshirt, and her favorite sneakers, Mary put the finishing touches on the Daddy-Daughter scrapbook she'd made for her father. It had long been a Landry family tradition between her parents and two siblings to exchange handmade gifts at Christmas. With her brother and sister both married, the practice had expanded to include spouses and Mary's two nephews and three nieces. Of course, she bought the little ones toys, too, but handmade gifts where the ones that mattered for the adults.

Eliza strolled into her office, carrying two crystal flutes in her right hand and a green bottle in her left. She set the glasses on Mary's desk and went about the business of opening the champagne. "Sorry I took so long. John called to grovel about missing the party, so I let him do it even though I totally support his job. I knew what I was in for when I fell for an obstetrician."

"Did his patient have her babies?"

"She did. Mama and triplets are doing great."

"Excellent."

Eliza filled two glasses with the sparkling wine, handed one to Mary, then raised her glass in a toast. "Merry Christmas, BFF."

"Merry Christmas. I hope you and John have a fabulous time in Hawaii."

"How can we not? Ten days of sun and sand, just the two of us, totally unplugged? It'll be heaven."

"The unplugged part sounds like heaven," Mary agreed.

"You're such a traditionalist, Mary."

"And unapologetic about it. For me, Christmas wouldn't be Christmas without all the trappings. I want family around me, bubble lights on the tree, and carols on the sound system. I want cookies to decorate and big fluffy bows on gifts. I want midnight mass and hot apple cider and 'It's a Wonderful Life' and sleigh rides. And I want snow!"

Eliza clinked her glass with Mary's. "And this is the difference between a girl born and raised in south Texas and one who grew up in the Rocky Mountains. So, when are you planning to leave for Colorado?"

"With any luck, first thing tomorrow morning." Mary sipped her champagne, then set it down. She checked the finishing touch on the scrapbook with her fingertip. The miniature fishing creel placed at the corner of a twenty-year-old photo of her father fishing with his three children in Rocky Mountain National Park was nice and dry. It was safe to close the book. Mary needed to wrap it and the two hard-cover novels containing the handmade gift IOU's she was giving her brother and sister before she headed home. Her sibs understood her busy season and would be happy with better-late-than-never, thank goodness.

"In other good news, I finally found a dog sitter for Angel. Jason Elliott told me tonight he'd take her. He just needs to clear it with his roommate. He said he'd call me tonight if there was a problem, and my phone hasn't rung."

On cue, Mary's cell phone rang.

It lay pushed to the side of her desk in its seasonal decorative Santa case. Her ring tone of choice for December was "White Christmas," and for the first time in Mary's life, the sound of Bing Crosby's voice didn't make her happy. She closed her eyes and whimpered a little as she reached to answer. "Hello?"

Two and a half minutes later, she disconnected the call, buried her head in her hands, and groaned.

Eliza set a champagne flute in front of her. "No room at Jason's inn, either, I take it?"

"No. Jason was my last hope. There's no other option. I've called every vet, every boarding facility, pet hotel, and pet sitter within fifty miles. Everything is full and has a waitlist. Nobody is offering me any hope that Angel will find a bed for Christmas."

Eliza winced. She took a sip of her drink and then pursed her lips and pondered a moment. "You asked Sarah?"

"Yes. And Linda, April, José, Kiley, Kenisha, Sam, Father Tom, Reverend Jenkins, Officer Larimer…"

"The butcher, the baker, and the candlestick maker?"

"Them, too."

"I'm sorry, sweets. You'd know I'd help if John and I weren't leaving for Hawaii tomorrow. I suppose it wouldn't be kind of me to say I told you so when you said yes to Wags and Walks?"

Mary chastised her partner with a look.

Eliza lifted her champagne in a toast. "Honey, you know I love dogs as much as anybody, and I think the work you do for Wags and Walks Rescue qualifies you for sainthood. But that dog…"

"She's an angel," Mary defended. "She's aptly named."

"Unfortunately, people aren't any different about choosing their pets than they are about choosing their partners. I'm afraid you might be stuck with that dog for a long time. Appearance matters. Note that you didn't choose to name her "Beauty" when the other volunteer pulled her from the pound and then dumped her on you at the last minute."

Mary brought her chin up. "Beauty is in the eyes of the beholder. Angel's forever family will see past her…challenges…to her sweet personality. I simply haven't had time to find them. Besides, it's not like I didn't know that I was taking on a special case when I let Rhonda Blankenship leave her with me."

"I know. I know. But I also witnessed your call to the rescue director. I heard her swear on her mother's grave that she would find a dog sitter over Christmas if you agreed to step in for Rhonda and take the new dog."

Mary shrugged. "Things happen."

"Right. And women elope and bail on commitments at the last minute all the time. So where did Rhonda and her new husband move to again?"

"Yap. It's an island in the South Pacific. It's supposed to be beautiful."

Eliza rolled her eyes and drawled, "I hope they'll be very happy. So that's it, then? You have no choice but to take that poor, pitiful, diarrhetic dog with you on a fourteen-hour car trip, then foist her off on your parents for two weeks? They're going to love that."

"They won't mind. Much. They're both dog lovers, although Mom does prefer little dogs."

"Nothing about Angel is little. She's a horse. A big, hairy horse."

"She's a big dog, yes, but don't forget she's carrying extra weight."

"I don't see how, considering that she tosses her cookies every time she eats. Oh, Mary. I'm going to worry about your road-warrioring in a seen-better-days Ford uphill through the blizzard with only a big, ugly, sick dog for company."

Mary gave her friend a chastising look. "Number one, my car might have a lot of miles, but it runs like a champ. Number two, I'm going to pretend I didn't hear the U-word. Number three, I've checked the travel conditions between Dallas and Eternity Springs, and nobody is predicting a blizzard to hit in the next two days. It's two to four inches of snow at the most once I reach the mountains, and I'll most likely be home before it starts. Number four, Angel isn't sick. The pregnancy has given her a sensitive digestive system. And finally, number five, I forbid you to spend one minute thinking about me, much less worrying. I expect you to devote all your time and attention to wringing every bit of comfort and joy from your romantic Christmas vacation with Dr. Hottie. And, to assist in that endeavor, I have a little something for you."

Mary opened one of her desk drawers and removed the small, wrapped package she'd placed there earlier.

"Mary!" Eliza exclaimed. "We already exchanged gifts. I love, love, love, love the organizer you gave me."

"I'm glad. This is a little something extra. It's my heart gift."

Eliza's eyes widened. Her voice held a note of wonder as she accepted the box, saying, "But…you didn't have time this year. You've only just finished your dad's gift. You're giving your siblings IOU's. You didn't even have time for the big fat family tradition event that's so important to you, your 'Gift of Giving to a Stranger.' But you took the time to make something for me?"

Mary could have pointed out how Eliza never failed to be there for her during the breakup with Travis. She could have talked about their excellent working relationship or the way Eliza always made her laugh when Mary really needed a laugh. But instead, she simply said, "You're my best friend, Eliza."

Her best friend burst out in uncharacteristic tears and tore into her present. "Booties! You knitted booties for me!"

"For the plane ride."

"Because I always kick my shoes off, and my feet always freeze. They're so soft. They're like a turquoise cloud. They're perfect. Thank you, Mary. I love them." Eliza threw her arms around her friend and gave her a hard hug. "There's only one problem. No way I won't think about you when I'm wearing them."

"Fair enough. You have permission to think about me only while you're sitting in First Class, wearing my booties, and sipping a Mai Tai."

"It's a deal. I'll drink a toast to you and Angel and tap my turquoise heels three times and wish you safely home over the river and through the woods without encountering a tornado or a blizzard or a cat named Toto."

"No cats. Angel doesn't care for cats."

Both women turned at the sound of the loading dock's buzzer. The cleanup crew had arrived. Eliza took one last sip of her champagne and set down the flute. "I've got the after-party. Consider it my heart gift to you. Stay here and wrap your presents, then go home and get a good night's sleep so that you and Angel can get an early start in the morning."

Mary accepted the gift in the spirit it was offered, and she gave her friend one more hug. "Thank you. Merry Christmas, Eliza."

"Merry Christmas, Mary." Booties in hand and whistling "I Saw Mommy Kissing Santa Claus," she left the office. A minute later, she ducked back inside and tossed something toward Mary, saying, "Since you're so big on Christmas traditions, I think you should stick this in your purse."

Jingle bells jangled as Mary caught the red ribbon holding the sprig of mistletoe that had been part of their decoration.

Eliza said, "You want to be the Girl Scout Elf when you're out walking Angel and run into Santa Hunk. Always prepared, you know."

"Santa Hunk?

"I know you are spending Christmas in a small, isolated

town with a shortage of single guys, but hey, it's the season of miracles, right? Put it in your purse, Mary."

Mary laughed, did as she was told, then returned to her gift wrapping. She finished up quickly. After checking with her partner, who assured her that everything was under control, she headed home to bed.

Mary dreamed vividly that night. Snow swirled in peppermint scented air, but there were no clouds in the inky blue sky, only a full moon and a million stars. She was flying. She was flying in a sleigh pulled by reindeer—with Angel in Rudolf's lead position. Angel's nose glowed red, and around her neck hung a St. Bernard's cask of brandy. Bing Crosby crooned about a white Christmas from the sleigh's sound system speakers.

Mary wore her green Christmas party dress, a red felt hat with jingle bells and pointed tip, and sparkling Judy Garland ruby slippers with curled, pointy toes. Was the curl because they were elf shoes, or because mistletoe hung above the sleigh, and Santa Hunk had kissed her all across the Pacific?

When the sleigh sailed past an airliner headed toward Hawaii, she came up for air long enough to give Eliza a beauty queen wave. Eliza lifted her Mai Tai in a toast.

Mary awoke with a smile on her face.

As a rule, she wasn't one to put any stock in the notion that dreams foretold the future. Still, right before she backed her loaded-up eight-year-old Ford Explorer out of the driveway, she added a new song to her playlist for the trip.

Mary Landry headed home to Eternity Springs, Colorado, for Christmas, singing along to "Santa Baby."

ALSO BY EMILY MARCH

Celebrate Eternity Springs Novellas

THE CHRISTMAS PAWDCAST

THE SUMMER MELT

Lake in the Clouds Women's Fiction Series

THE GETAWAY

The Brazos Bend Contemporary Romance Series

MY BIG OLD TEXAS HEARTACHE

THE LAST BACHELOR IN TEXAS

The Callahan Brothers Trilogy

LUKE—The Callahan Brothers

MATT—The Callahan Brothers

MARK—The Callahan Brothers

A CALLAHAN CAROL

The Eternity Springs Contemporary Romance Series

ANGEL'S REST

HUMMINGBIRD LAKE

HEARTACHE FALLS

LOVER'S LEAP

NIGHTINGALE WAY

REFLECTION POINT

MIRACLE ROAD

DREAMWEAVER TRAIL

TEARDROP LANE

HEARTSONG COTTAGE

REUNION PASS

CHRISTMAS IN ETERNITY SPRINGS

A STARDANCE SUMMER

THE FIRST KISS OF SPRING

THE CHRISTMAS WISHING TREE

The Eternity Springs: McBrides of Texas Trilogy

JACKSON

TUCKER

BOONE

Celebrate Eternity Springs Novella Collection

THE CHRISTMAS PAWDCAST novella

BETTER THAN A BOX OF CHOCOLATES novella

THE SUMMER MELT novella

And, SEASON OF SISTERS, a stand alone women's fiction novel.

The Bad Luck Wedding Historical Romance Series

THE BAD LUCK WEDDING DRESS

THE BAD LUCK WEDDING CAKE

Bad Luck Abroad Trilogy

SIMMER ALL NIGHT

SIZZLE ALL DAY

THE BAD LUCK WEDDING NIGHT

Bad Luck Brides Quartet

HER BODYGUARD

HER SCOUNDREL

HER OUTLAW

THE LONER

Stand Alone Historical Romances

THE TEXAN'S BRIDE

CAPTURE THE NIGHT

THE SCOUNDREL'S BRIDE

THE WEDDING RANSOM

THE COWBOY'S RUNAWAY BRIDE

ABOUT THE AUTHOR

Emily March is the *New York Times, Publishers Weekly*, and *USA Today* bestselling author of over forty novels, including the critically acclaimed Eternity Springs series. Publishers Weekly calls March a "master of delightful banter," and her heartwarming, emotionally charged stories have been named to Best of the Year lists by *Publishers Weekly, Library Journal,* and Romance Writers of America. A graduate of Texas A&M University, Emily is an avid fan of Aggie sports and her recipe for jalapeño relish has made her a tailgating legend.